CW01499732

ACKNOWLEDGEMENTS

I have harassed, harried and continually pestered many people during the writing of this book, the first in a trilogy of crime novels set in my hometown of Warrington.
I am lucky enough to have friends and relatives who are, or have been police officers, their help and observations were invaluable during the creative process.
I would especially like to mention Roy, who was one of my beta readers and gave me an unbiased appraisal of the book. Roy has known me most of my life and was slightly shocked that I could be
'so gruesome!'
Maggie, who read the book for me and her husband Jack, also a police officer who gave me some tips from a C I D perspective which were very useful indeed.
And Brian, who is an ex-police officer and fellow writer, and has at his fingertips, a host of software, documents and web sites to offer in the way of guidance.
To my editor Liz Hedgecock who puts up with all my late-night messages when something has gone wrong, her patience is extraordinary.
To my youngest son Jon, who is my IT guru, as I am the original technophobe. He should get a medal for helping his mum again, and again because I am so technically dyslexic.
And last, but not least, to all my readers, you five know who you are, a big thanks you. There would be no point

without you.

DEDICATION

For my husband David. Without you
I couldn't do 'my thing.'

BE VERY CAREFUL, THEN, HOW YOU LIVE-NOT AS UNWISEBUT AS WISE, MAKING THE MOST OF EVERY OPPORTUNITYBECAUSE THE DAYS ARE EVIL.

Ephesians 5:15-16

PROLOGUE

He stood back to admire his work. It was good. Not perfect, but good. He smiled and gently touched a hand.

Would the investigating officer suspect this was his first time? That he was a murder virgin?

What did it matter? He was proving a point, and all he had to do now was get away with it. That would show those idiots who had scoffed at his brilliant ideas.

The hands and feet had been tougher to remove than he thought. The face, though, had been easy.

Now he just needed a place for the body to be found, and then he could sit back and watch the circus from a distance.

This was going to be fun.

1.

Detective Inspector Wen Price ducked under the police tape at the small shopping precinct in Penketh and looked at the hive of activity before her. Men and women scurried about in white suits, with blue gloves and overshoes just to make the whole ensemble more on-trend.

'What have we got, Cassie?' she asked as she approached the young detective sergeant.

Cassie Rowden turned to her boss. 'Male, found about an hour ago in one of the big bins by a shop owner. No ID, no clothes, no hands and feet. Not much face left, come to that.'

'What?'

'It's messy this one, ma'am.'

'When is murder not messy, Cassie?'

Eight o'clock in the morning, on what should have been a beautiful spring day in this area of Cheshire, had now turned into a bleak murder scene.

Wen pulled on overshoes and grabbed a mask from a plastic box at the side of the white tent which shielded the general public from the grisly scene, and the SOCO team from the bloodthirsty public.

She popped her head inside the tent to see what was going on, and even she felt nausea rising with the sight of the corpse. At the head, suited and booted, knelt pathologist John Baron. 'Hi, John. First thoughts?'

'Morning, Wen. And how are we today?'

'Trying to keep my piece of toast down at the moment. That's a bloody mess.'

'And how. The face has been smashed to a pulp. Somebody has anger issues, if you ask me.'

'I didn't.' John looked at her over his protective goggles, and she could see from the way his eyes crinkled that he was smiling at her. 'What can you tell me?'

'Male, between twenty-five and thirty-five. He's been dead about twelve hours, he wasn't killed here, and he's had his hands and feet removed.'

'Strangely enough, I had noticed that little detail,' said Wen. 'He was murdered on Wednesday then.'

'Yep, and it wasn't a clean job; a bit of hacking's been done. Probably didn't have the right equipment is my guess.'

'OK. When are you doing the PM?' Wen looked at her watch.

'Later today. You going to be there?'

'No, it'll be Cassie. I've got to be in court.'

'I'll look forward to your padawan accompanying me in your absence.'

Wen wondered if John, a massive sci-fi fan, would be happier doing his PMs with a lightsabre. 'Yeah, right.' She turned to go.

'Oh, and Wen?'

'Yes?'

'May the force be with you.'

'Geek!'

She went to find her sergeant, who was deep in conversation with a uniformed officer. 'Cassie?'

'Yes, boss?'

'PM later.'

'Great!' Cassie looked at the floor and kicked a stone.

'I'm in court,' she clarified, not wanting her DS to think she was pulling rank to duck out of the dicing and slicing. Since their DCI had gone off sick, Wen's workload had doubled. The gap would soon be filled, she had been told. But she had heard that before. 'For starters I want all these bins emptied and the contents bagging.'

'All of them?'

'Yes. And a door-to-door done. Any CCTV around here?'

'At the front of the shops, but none round the back here.'

The area was a square with shops on three sides, and a car park on the fourth.

'What about that light?' Wen pointed at a security light sensor on the corner of the building.

'Not working. Hasn't worked for months, apparently.'

'And the guy that found him?'

'In his shop. He's feeling slightly lightheaded as his breakfast ended up all over the tarmac.'

'Right, I'll go and have a word.' And with that Wen strode off in search of her body finder.

***

'Mr...?'

'Garnet. Peter Garnet.' The man stood at the his shop door looking distracted.

Wen looked at the man and wondered if he was always this pale, or whether it was just shock. The witness looked about mid-forties, and probably smoked as many cigarettes as he sold if his quiet wheeze was anything to go by. 'Mr Garnet, I'm Detective Inspector Price. Can you tell me what happened, please?'

'Do I have to? I've already told at least three people.' He pulled hard on his cigarette.

'Please. I'd like to hear it for myself.'

He smiled, but it was strained, 'it's true, you know.'

'What is?'

'That you're getting old when the police start looking young. And you're a detective inspector. You look more like a model.'

Wen blushed. Being tall, blonde and slim actually had its drawbacks at times. Times like these, when you needed to be taken seriously about something so heinous. 'Right,' she said, trying to ignore what was probably meant as a compliment. 'Shall we sit down?'

They went into the back room of the newsagent's. It was a small area with tea-making paraphernalia, two easy chairs and a sink. In one corner was a small toilet cubicle. They both took a chair. 'So, from the beginning, please.'

He sighed. 'All right. I came in early to do some stocking-up and some accounts. When I'd unpacked the cigarettes and today's papers, I put the kettle on and took my rubbish to the bin.'

'Through the back door?'

'Yeah. I threw the cardboard into the blue bin, but it just slid out again. I thought that was strange, because there was plenty of room yesterday, so I stood on an old beer crate to push the rubbish down, and that's when I saw him.' He swallowed hard at the memory of his macabre find. Wen suspected Peter Garnet would need a whole heap of therapy before he would sleep at night again.

'Am I right in thinking that those bins are shared by all the shops?'

'Yes, each row has the same set up. For recycling, and that. Not sure what colour it should be for recycling bodies, though.' He rubbed the back of his neck and took a deep breath.

Wen smiled. 'No, I wouldn't know that either. What time do you open for business?'

'About seven. People come for cigs and newspapers on their way to work. My takings are good between seven and nine.'

'Have you seen anybody about recently who made you feel nervous, or apprehensive? No one hanging around looking shifty when you locked up last night?'

Mr Garnet shook his head.

'All right,' said Wen. 'If you think of anything, or a customer says anything to you once the news gets out, can you let us know?'

'Yes, of course. Can I open today?' he asked hopefully.

'No, sorry. It's a crime scene; well, the back is. We'll be as quick as possible, but this is a no-go area for the rest of today.' Wen looked at the shopkeeper. 'To be honest, I think you should go home, anyway. You've had a hell of a shock.'

'I'd rather work, actually. Take my mind off it.' He put his hand to his brow and rubbed the area over his nose, then turned to Wen. 'Who would do that? Why would someone do that? It was barbaric. The face, it had gone. This is Warrington, not downtown New York.'

Wen left Mr Garnet smoking another cigarette, ignoring the spasm of coughing it had stimulated. She never told people smoking was bad for their health; not when she worked with death and murder on a regular basis. Most of her team smoked. Either that, or they drank too much, or both. And who could blame them? Not her.

***

Back at base, Wen was putting finishing touches to a murder board, ready for the team briefing the next morning. Hopefully by then they would have slightly more information than they had now. Just then her IT guru came into the room on crutches.

'Jake, whatever you were going to do, forget it. Missing persons for the last four weeks. Male, between twenty and forty. Start in a ten-mile area from here, then expand to fifteen.'

'Yes, ma'am.'

'And Jake, email the team. Briefing here at eight tomorrow morning.'

'Yes, ma'am.'

'And Jake...'

This time the young officer just looked at Wen, as if to say, 'What else?'

'How's the leg?'

'Oh. Getting there, thank you, ma'am.' He sank down gratefully into his chair, propping his crutches to one side.

'I hope you're getting rid of that bike?'

'That's what my mum tells me.'

'Good. Listen to her, mums know best.'

As she left the building, Wen smiled at the absurdity of her advice. As if she would ever have any idea what a mum might know.

She had two hours before she needed to be at Manchester Crown Court. Just enough time to grab some lunch, shower and change, and then get the one o'clock train from Central Station.

As Wen drove up to the Grade 2-listed detached house on the outskirts of the town, she knew that her lunch would be on the table by the time she made it into the kitchen. There was no way a car could come up their gravel drive quietly. One of the main reasons they had never got rid of it was that it acted as an early warning system. Not just for herself, but more importantly the other member of the household, her twin brother Aran. Brother and sister, both tall and slim with blond hair, there was no escape from the fact they shared the same genes.

As Wen entered the hall she noticed that her scarf, which she had left there yesterday, had not been moved. She crossed into the kitchen where Aran was placing a plate on a mat, ready for her to sit down and eat.

'No Mrs G?' Wen asked.

'She's ill. Been sick, so I told her not to come back until she is completely well again.'

'And how long will that be?'

'At least twenty-four hours after she vomits for the last time.' Aran hadn't looked at his sister during this conversation, too busy loading the dishwasher to be distracted by the presence of his twin.

Their kitchen was large enough to take a comfortable settee, large farmhouse table and six chairs, though Wen couldn't remember the last time more than two chairs were used at the same time. But it was a homely room, and it was where she spent most of her time when she was here.

'This looks nice.' Wen picked up her knife and fork and made a start on her mixed beans and feta cheese salad, wishing it was a cheese and pickle sandwich. 'Aren't you eating?'

'Not yet. You know you'll have to do some housework, don't you?' Aran asked.

'Yes, but —'

'No buts, Arwen. Those are the rules. If Mrs Guess can't come in, you must do the housework. I do my rooms and the kitchen.'

Wen knew she couldn't argue. 'I will, Aran, but we have a murder inquiry as from this morning and I might be a bit busy for the foreseeable.'

Aran tutted. 'Well, I'm not doing it.'

'I don't expect you to. I'll do it, but you'll have to give me a little leeway.'

'That's convenient, isn't it?' Aran gave Wen a quick glance of disapproval, 'Mrs Guess goes off sick, and suddenly you have a murder.'

'I'm sorry, Aran, but I don't think this chap decided to get killed so I'd have an excuse not to tidy the house.' Wen got a nod from her brother, but she wasn't sure he believed her.

Thirty minutes later Wen was heading out again, with a clean suit on and indigestion. As she got into her car she thought, not for the first time, that this place was far too big for just the two of them. It had four bedrooms, two of which Aran had made his; a large bedroom with an en suite, and a sitting room/study which he seldom left. Wen had the master suite plus the rest of the house to rattle around in. But it had been their parents' house, and their grandparents' before them, and according to Aran, they had to stay. So stay they did.

2.

Cassie made coffee, and Jake went to the canteen to fetch bacon butties for the team. Early morning starts were always like this. You could say what you liked about their DI, but she believed in teamwork and she treated her team well — as long as they did what they were supposed to.

Cassie had seen Wen take a DS apart once because he had cocked up big-style on a case. He'd fallen asleep during surveillance and let the prime suspect get away with murder right under his nose. The suspect had managed to get rid of crucial evidence, and therefore the CPS couldn't even get it to court. That DS had gone elsewhere, and Cassie had replaced him by getting her sergeant's exam just at the right moment. So far she had enjoyed her time in the Cheshire Serious Crime Squad and found her DI hardworking and thorough. That was also what she expected from her team.

Of course Wen was there before anyone else, and no one could sneak in without being named and shamed. 'It's all right for her,' said a female detective, who had been blasted on more than one occasion for turning up late due to childcare issues. 'She's got no family. Just this fucking job.'

Who exactly did the DI have waiting for her at home? No one really knew. Someone had said she had a handicapped brother to look out for, but even that was conjecture.

Wen surveyed the room. 'Right, have we all got refreshments?'

Nods all round.

'Excellent, then I'll begin.' Wen turned to the whiteboard. 'Right. What do we know then? Sod all, that's what. Anything from the door to door?'

'No, boss,' one of her officers said, 'no one saw nothing or heard nothing. Except a cat fight about two in the morning, that is.'

Wen winced at the Detective Constable's explanation of the situation, not to mention his poor use of the English language. That was what happened when you lived with someone who had a master's degree in English Literature. 'No cars noticed, or heard? Nothing?'

'No, boss.'

'What about the PM, Cassie? Did that throw any light on the mode of death?'

'Nothing of note on the torso, ma'am, so the Bloody Red Baron suspects it was a head wound that did for him.'

Wen spun round. 'Don't call the doctor that in front of me, do you understand?'

'Sorry ma'am, but everyone calls him that —'

'Not when I can hear them they don't. We all deserve the respect of our colleagues, Cassie, and I won't have you or anyone else disrespect anyone on my team. If you want to call each other stupid names, that just shows the infantile side of your nature.' Wen turned back to the board, knowing full well that faces were being pulled behind her. God alone knew what they called her, but as long as she didn't hear what they said, she didn't care. 'What about DNA?'

'He's on to that. Be a few days before he gets that back, though.'

Cassie had quickly regained her equilibrium, Wen noticed, which was good. That was another thing she really couldn't stand: sulky staff. How many times over the years had *she* been made a show of? Too many. But she learned the lesson, and moved on. 'Any ideas why he took his feet? His hands I can understand, but his feet?' She paused, but there was silence. 'Anyone?'

Cassie spoke up again. 'The doc thinks there might have been a deformity or a tattoo which would have helped with ID. But that's just a guess.'

'Jake, anyone of interest missing locally?'

'Just two in the last few weeks who meet our criteria.

A thirty-year-old from Frodsham, Paul James. He went off to some sort of folk music evening on Friday night, and his partner hasn't seen him since.'

'And that's unusual, is it?'

'Yes, and no.' Jake surveyed the room. Every eye was upon him, every ear listening. The floor was his. Wen had realised when Jake came to work for her that he was a show-off. That was probably why he had ended up on life support after a motorbike accident. But he was also very good at his job, and he knew it.

'Well come on, boy wonder, don't leave us hanging,' she said.

'His boyfriend says he's done this before; gone on a night out and just disappeared for days at a time.'

'And?'

'And I wondered why this time it was different. So I got in touch with the local force and they said that he's never been reported missing before. They have been called to that address once, though. To a domestic.'

'So why has he reported him missing this time?' Wen said this as she wrote notes on the whiteboard.

'Exactly!' Jake looked around the room as if expecting applause. When it wasn't forthcoming, he continued. 'The other is a Polish lad, Vlad Mlyoski, who works at a local car wash. Didn't go home to his girlfriend on Saturday evening after work. The problem here is that he is an illegal, so he could have done a flit because he thought immigration were on to him.'

'But his girlfriend obviously has other ideas?' queried Wen.

'Yep. She's here legally and said Vlad was waiting for his papers, and he wouldn't have just gone. She reported him because, and I quote, bad men are wanting him, unquote.'

'Interesting. Good work, Jake. Keep on it, and see what else you can find. Right. Richard and Becky, get yourselves over to sunny Frodsham and question this lad's boyfriend. I want some DNA from that house. Hair, toothbrush, whatever. Try and talk to the neighbours and see if they have heard any rucks lately. OK?' The two detectives nodded affirmation. 'Jake, flag up Paul's name at local A&Es and minor injuries units and see if he's attended with any injuries in the last year or two. And Cassie, come with me. My car needs cleaning.'

***

As they pulled into the car wash Cassie parked in one of the waiting bays. 'No, you can go straight to car wash,' said a tall man with a goatee beard as he walked away from a girl he'd been talking to as they drove in.

Instead, Wen and Cassie got out of their vehicle. 'We don't need a car wash today, thanks.'

'Who are you? What you want?' He advanced on Wen, looking slightly threatening.

She took her ID out of her pocket. 'DI Price, and this is my sergeant.'

'We are all legal here.' He looked as if he might want to spit on them.

'We're not from immigration, Mr...'

'Mazur, Jan Mazur. So, what do you want?'

'We're looking for a man called Vlad Mlyoski. Can we speak to him, please?'

'No one here of that name.' He turned to walk away.

'But he worked here until recently.' The Detective inspector smiled.

'No.'

Wen looked at Cassie, who stepped forward. 'Mr Mazur, we have it on good authority that this man worked for you. We know he didn't have any papers, and we aren't interested in that, but it's important that we trace him.' She then smiled, knowing this always threw people.

'I don't know this man. Now please, go.'

Cassie stepped even closer, this time invading Jan's personal space. 'This is a murder inquiry, sir. If you don't co-operate with us, we will have no alternative but to take your whole workforce in for questioning, and bring in our very good friend from immigration. And he will examine all your papers and dealings with a very big magnifying glass. Do you understand me?'

This time he just nodded.

'So,' said Wen. 'when did you last see him?'

'Saturday. He did an eight till eight shift and then left. Didn't turn up for work next day.'

'There now, that wasn't hard, was it?' Wen made some notes in her pocketbook.

'What has he done?' Jan spoke over Cassie's head to Wen.

'Nothing, as far as we know. Was he afraid of anyone, or did someone hold a grudge against him?' Wen tried to keep eye contact with Jan.

The man just shook his head this time.

'And how long did he work for you?' Wen asked the questions but Cassie stood stock still looking at the man.

'Hard to say. They come and they go.'

'A ballpark figure, then.' Cassie had folded her arms, and wasn't moving until she had an answer.

'Two, three months.'

'Thank you so much, Mr Mazur,' said Wen. 'We will be in touch. And if you hear anything from Vlad please let us know at once.' Wen handed the man her card and walked away, followed by Cassie who had given him one last long look. He yelled in what sounded like Polish at the girl he had been talking to earlier, and retreated into a tiny hut. Wen suspected that Jan didn't like being told what to do, especially by a woman.

In her peripheral vision she saw the small dark girl bob down and pick something up from the tarmac where they had been standing.

'Excuse!' she shouted, as she ran after them. Wen turned to face her. 'You drop this,' she said, holding out a scrap of paper.

'I don't...'

'Yes, you drop this,' said the girl imploringly.

'Oh, yes. Of course. Thank you so much.' She took the note and watched the girl go back to the hut, glancing once at them with a quick smile.

Wen and Cassie got back in the car, and as they pulled away Wen opened the scrap of paper. On it was written an address and a time: 9pm. 'Guess me and you are on overtime tonight, Cassie,' said Wen.

***

In Frodsham, Becky Wainwright knocked on the door of a very nice terraced cottage on the main street. Richard was speaking to Jake on his phone. 'Thanks mate, that's very interesting. Catch you later.'

'What's very interesting?' said Becky.

'About the A&E visits...'

'What about them?'

Just then the door was opened by a dejected-looking individual, tall, lanky, and wearing a robe over his vest and pants. 'Yes?'

'Mr Wall?'

'Yes. What do you want? If it's God you're trying to sell me, you can fuck off, because you know what, there is no fucking God.'

Becky and Richard produced their ID at the same time, like well-practised magicians. 'DC Wainwright and DC Jones, Mr Wall, from Cheshire Serious Crime Squad. We would like to talk to you about Paul James.'

With that the man crumpled to the floor. 'Oh God, oh God, he's dead, isn't he? Oh, dear God!'

As they helped Mr Wall into the house Becky reflected on how many times people renounced the Almighty, only to reinstate him when they needed help. As he slumped in an armchair, sobbing, the two detectives looked at each other. 'Mr Wall, we have no reason to think that Paul is dead.'

He looked up. 'Then what are you doing here?'

'We are making inquiries into a case, and we need to eliminate some missing men.'

'What sort of case?'

'Have you a recent photo of Paul which we could borrow?' asked Becky. She could see the man falling to pieces in front of them, and wanted to halt the process by giving him something else to think about, something to do. 'And a hairbrush, maybe?'

'What? Yes.' He began to get up.

'It can wait until later, Mr Wall,' said Richard. 'First, can I ask why you reported Paul as a missing person?' Richard sat down close to the man, leaning towards him and making his body language friendly. 'You told the local police that he's done this sort of thing before. What was different this time?'

'The other times...' Mr Wall looked very uncomfortable. 'The other times were when we had quarrelled. This time we were OK. We've turned a corner. We're happy.'

'Did you hit your boyfriend, Mr Wall?' said Becky, glaring at him.

'What! No! I would never hit Paul, never!' He pulled at the material of his robe in a distracted way.

'No,' said Richard. 'But he's beaten you up, hasn't he?'

'What?' cried Becky, staring at her partner.

'He didn't mean to,' said Mr Wall. 'He has... He has issues, but he's been getting help.'

'Now let me get this straight,' Becky said. 'In the past he's gone walkabout after physically assaulting you?'

'It wasn't that bad.'

Richard unlocked his phone, opened his emails, and read an extract from what Jake had just sent him. 'A fractured cheekbone, four fractured ribs, one concussion—'

'Stop! Please just stop.' The man looked at the floor. 'I love him, and he didn't come home on Friday after we'd had a wonderful day together. I'd cooked supper and we were going to watch a movie when he got back from the gig. But he didn't. Didn't get back, I mean.' He started crying again.

'You didn't go with him,' said Becky. 'Why was that?'

Mr Wall stared at her. 'Folk music? I'd rather stick pins in my eyes.'

'Fair answer,' said Richard, who thought the only music worth listening to was rock.

'OK, Mr Wall, let's take a full description.' Becky got out her pocketbook, feeling that they might be on to something here.

3.

Cassie parked the unmarked police car on the road, they were in part of a depressing housing estate in a less than salubrious area of the town. She knocked on the door of the address they'd been given by the car-wash girl. Curtains hung haphazardly from dirty windows, and the paint was peeling off the door frame in an attempt to escape.

As soon as Cassie took her hand away from the wood vicious barking started, and feet galloped over a hard floor like heavy hailstones hitting a metal roof. 'Just what I need!' she cried as she backed away.

'Not a fan of our four-legged friends then, Cassie?' asked Wen as she stepped in front of her.

'Not unless they work for their living, and I'm definitely not a fan of the sort that can bite your head off.'

A foreign voice shouted something, and the barking ceased. Then the door opened as much as the safety chain would allow, showing a slobbering, large-jawed canine being held back by the small hand of their contact. 'Moment.' She disappeared with her protector, then returned and let them in.

'Dog?' Cassie poked her head around the door.

'In the kitchen. Come.' She indicated the front room. It was small, dark, and smelt of body odour. On the floor were two single mattresses and sleeping bags. The general clutter made the place look more like a squat than anything else.

'Are you alone?' asked Wen.

The girl nodded.

'It's Anna, isn't it?' Wen sat down on the edge of one of the chairs, hoping not to stain her jacket. 'OK, Anna, you reported your boyfriend missing, so tell us why you are worried about Vlad.'

'He didn't come home to me. He didn't come home.' Anna sank down on a battered old settee and sniffled.

Cassie went to sit next to her. 'Anna, could he have run away because he thought he might get deported?'

'Not without me. He made a promise. He say if he had to leave, we would go together.'

Wen studied her. 'Who did you mean when you said bad men were after him?'

'They want money. They say he owe them money.'

'What for?' This time Anna looked down at her feet rather than answering Wen. 'Anna, why did he owe money? Was it for getting him here, to this country?'

'No, he paid that. All he earns went to that.'

'So what was it, then?' Wen persisted.

'He is grammbler.'

'Grammbler? Do you mean gambler?'

'Yes. He won first. Then not.'

'And these people, did they lend him money to bet with?' Cassie put her hand over the girl's.

'Yes, I think. Vlad would not talk, but he was afraid.'

'Do you know who these people are?' the DI asked.

Anna looked at Wen, and shook her head.

'Have you got a recent photo of Vlad?' Cassie smiled at the girl.

Anna took out her phone and after a moment showed one to the sergeant. 'That's good,' said Cassie. 'Can I forward this to our office, and then we'll all know what he looks like.' She reluctantly handed her phone to Cassie. 'And have you got a comb or toothbrush that belongs to Vlad?'

Anna looked at Wen as if she had gone mad. 'Why?'

'To see if we can get Vlad's DNA.' That didn't help; she looked even more confused than ever. 'It's a test that can help to identify people, sometimes.' Wen tried to explain, hoping that made some sort of sense to the girl.

Anna went upstairs, still not looking convinced, and while she was gone Cassie quickly scrolled through the text messages on her phone, but they were in Polish.

The girl reappeared with a blue toothbrush. 'Is it right?'

Cassie took an evidence bag out of her pocket. 'That's fine, just pop it in here.' She held the bag open and Anna dropped the brush inside. 'And nobody else has used this?'

'Nobody,' confirmed Anna.

'I'll just take a description of Vlad and then we'll leave you in peace.'

'But I told man on phone. Answered his questions.'

'Yes, but we just want to double check we have it right.' Wen always liked to watch people when they gave this sort of information. Over the years she had learned how to tell whether a person was genuinely worried, or just doing what was expected. Anna was genuinely worried.

The description taken, Wen handed the girl her card. 'If you hear from Vlad or think of anything else, anything at all, phone me.'

'How many others live here with you, Anna?' asked Cassie.

'Seven, until Vlad back, then eight.'

'Where are they all today?'

'Working.'

'How many men?' Cassie was worried about this arrangement.

'Five.'

'Does Jan live here?'

Anna shook her head.

'Are you safe here, Anna?' This time Wen asked the question.

'Yes, I have Bruno.'

'Bruno?'

'Yes, my dog.'

'Well, I'm glad you've got something to protect yourself with,' said Wen. 'We'll be in touch with any news.'

As they drove back to base, Wen suddenly said, 'No tattoos.'

'No,' replied Cassie. 'I thought all east Eastern European men had at least one.'

Wen thought. 'We shouldn't stereotype, should we.'
'No. but we do,' said her sergeant.

4.

The following morning, Cassie was doing the buttie run before the team briefing when she met John Baron. 'Morning, Cassie,' he said casually, as he held the canteen door open for her.

'Morning, doc.' She slid past him, trying to remember who wanted brown sauce and who wanted red.

'Oh, by the way,' he called after her. 'Nothing came up on the corpse's DNA. Nothing on file.'

'Right, I'll let them know.'

'Thanks, Cassie.'

'Oh, doc...'

He turned to face her. 'Yes?'

'Our DI.'

'Yes?'

'You know her better than anyone on the team.'

'Probably. Where's this going, Cassie? Not planning a surprise birthday party for her, are you?'

Cassie looked shocked. 'Oh God, is it her birthday?'

He grinned. 'No idea. Which tells you what I know about her; not much at all.'

'No, but more than we do.'

'Probably.'

'So, what's her backstory, doc?' Detective inspector Wen Price was an enigma to Cassie, and she didn't like that lack of information; after all, knowledge is power.

'Do you know what I think, Cassie?' John Baron looked slightly annoyed as he said this.

'What?'

'I think you should ask her yourself.'

'She won't tell *me* anything.' She shrugged her shoulders and smiled.

'And that's my point.' John Baron released the door, and

headed back to the safety of his lab.

***

The leads they had on the male victim now sitting in one of their cold cabinets were few and far between. The only fresh piece of information they had to go on was another possible missing male.

'This one is thirty-five,' said Jake. 'A Martin Grimes, who lives with his mother and went missing last Thursday. He has a history of mental instability and has done this before on several occasions, according to his mum, who is very worried about him.'

'Well, she's his mum.' Cassie said what everyone else was thinking.

'Yes, but he hasn't been taking his lithium, so she thinks he might do something stupid.' Jake had a superior look on his face which said, more plainly than words, 'I've got more information than you, so shut it.'

'What sort of stupid?' Wen asked.

'He tried to burn down a school once.'

Richard almost choked on his buttie. 'With kids in?'

'No, at night, thank God. Did a lot of damage though. He has also cut his wrists, taken an overdose, and tried to drown himself. Not all at the same time, obviously.'

'Obviously,' said Cassie sarcastically, arms folded across her chest.

'I would say his mum has got reason to be concerned,' Jake said smugly. Wouldn't you, Sarge?'

Wen got up from her seat. 'Right, I'll go and have a word with his mum. Becky, find out who his community psychiatric nurses are and talk to them. In the meantime, any leads on our other two lost boys?'

Before anyone could speak, a uniformed officer barged into the office. 'Don't you know to knock, constable?' Wen said wearily.

'Yes, ma'am. Sorry ma'am, but the desk sergeant said to come up straightaway and tell you.'

'Well, tell me then!' Wen barked.

'There's another body, ma'am, and this one's worse!'

**

This time Wen and her team beat SOCO by a good five minutes. She found herself in a local park, at a children's play area, looking at the body of a young woman hanging like a crucifixion from a climbing frame. Her abdomen had been opened, and her entrails drooped flaccidly, like meat in a butcher's window. As a final flourish, her eyes had been gouged out. Blood pooled on the ground below the body.

Wen didn't want to look at the corpse, but she couldn't drag her gaze away. 'Who discovered the body?' she asked, trying to think of this horrific sight as work, *her* work.

'A paperboy, at six this morning,' said the uniformed officer who had been the first one on the scene after the boy. 'He's been taken to hospital and they're treating him for shock.'

'I'm not surprised,' said Wen.

She managed to look away from the corpse as a white van turned up, closely followed by three other cars. John Baron emerged from one of the cars and immediately went to his boot and started dressing for the occasion. Wen walked towards him. 'We've got a problem,' she said, as he wriggled into his white suit.

John glanced at the scene. 'Not the same MO, though.'

'No. But since when have we had two sadistic murders within days, around here?'

'True. But let's not jump to any conclusions until we know more.'

Wen was glad of his voice of reason. 'I definitely need to know more. I'll be at this PM, John.' He nodded and grabbed his case, ready to start work on the poor soul now being covered by a screen.

'Right. Cassie,' Wen beckoned her sergeant over. 'Any CCTV in the vicinity, I want it viewed. We need as many uniforms as we can get to do a search from here in all directions. Richard and Becky, door-to-door on the nearest housing estate, please. Did anyone see or hear anything. Is anyone missing from the area.' She looked at her team. 'I'm going to the Chief; I think we have a serial killer on our hands.'

***

He watched from a distance, through the viewfinder. It was going well. They didn't have a clue about the first body, but he had left them more to work with this time. It would, however, point them in completely the wrong direction.

May be would leave the next one a week or so. The media would have a field day when they knew about this, and he would be the one to tell them.

***

'I think you're being a bit previous, Wen. A serial killer? Really?' Chief Inspector Charles Manning looked tense.

'I know what you're thinking, sir, but it's more than a co-incidence. Two brutal murders within a week, here in Warrington.'

'But these two bodies go against everything that points to a multiple murderer, Wen. You studied psychology, you know that. Serial killers have patterns. They go for the same type of victim, they kill in the same way.'

'I've just got a feeling that these two are linked. I was wondering—'

'I know what you're going to say, Wen, and the answer is no. Not yet, at any rate.' The Chief Inspector gave Wen the look of a man being backed into a corner. 'Three plus bodies before we can claim we might have a serial killer. You know that.'

Wen folded her arms. 'So we wait until another body turns up, do we?'

'No. We wait until we have more information before we call in Jeff Morgan.'

Wen exhaled. 'I think we need him now, sir.'

'Have you any idea how much a profiler costs?' the Chief demanded. 'If you had my budget, *you'd* hold off.'

Wen gave him a stern look. 'With respect, sir, I don't think money should come before public safety.'

'These murder inquiries are going to push expenditure anyway, you know that.' Wen held his gaze. 'Oh, for God's sake, all right.'

She smiled. 'Thank you, sir.'

'Just one day, for his opinion. Are you clear on that, Detective Inspector?'

'Sir.'

'And Wen...'

'Yes, sir?'

'Have you given any more thought to acting up as DCI?'

'Yes sir, and the answer is still no thank you, sir.'

'Why? We are having a job getting a temporary replacement for Marilyne Aldane. God alone knows how long she'll be off.'

'I don't want a promotion sir, not even a temporary one. I like where I am with my career for now.'

'Oh all right, but I won't give up asking you know.'

'Yes, sir.'

As she closed the Chief Inspector's door, Wen knew her boss understood why she couldn't take a promotion. But neither of them wanted to go there.

For now she had a more pressing problem: Jeff Morgan. Having him on the case was a double-edged sword. He was good, very good. But Wen hated him with a passion after what he had done to her.

5.

Jeff Morgan sat in his office at the University of Liverpool, quite aware of what was going on in Warrington. He was waiting for their call, so confident was he that they would need him sooner or later. Probably sooner.

It was a long time since he had worked with DI Price. The last time, it was obvious she still held a grudge against him. He hoped she had got over that by now. After all, it had been more than five years ago. And despite her cold attitude, he liked working with her. She was a good cop, and he enjoyed a challenge.

Last time they had worked together they solved a case of two missing children. Too late for one, but the second child had been reunited with his family. Jeff did wonder if the boy would thank them for that when he got older, because he was never going to get over what had happened to him. He was scarred physically and mentally, for life. In fact, Jeff wouldn't be at all surprised to see him as one of his patients in years to come. He hoped to God the child would get some sort of help, because he was going to need it.

A tap on his door meant that his two o'clock appointment had turned up. 'Yes, come in.'

A tall, well-built man peeped around the door. 'Come in, Tom.'

Tom eased himself into the room as if he were in a narrow tunnel and he suffered from claustrophobia. He stroked the outside of his thighs in a continual, nervous movement. 'It's OK, Tom. It's just you and me. Come and sit down.'

The man sat down. At no time since entering had he made eye contact with Jeff. Every muscle was taut, and he was ready to flee.

Jeff opened his notebook. 'Now, Tom, you were telling me last time about how you wanted to kill your mother. Shall we take it from there?'

***

Becky was fed up. Too much wine last night was now tapping her on the shoulder and telling her she needed coffee and painkillers. Just around the corner from the murder site was the middle-class suburb of Stockton Heath, with overpriced houses and too many cars. But it also had a collection of small boutiques, restaurants, and more importantly, coffee shops. Becky headed for one now.

It was cold and bright today; not the kind of weather for a grisly murder. Bluebells and daffodils were poking their heads above ground to see if they could come out to play yet.

The first coffee emporium she saw was called 24/7, so she went in. The bell rang as she entered, and the welcome smell of coffee beans made her mouth fill with saliva.

'Morning, what can I do for you?' The man behind the counter was as bright and cheerful as the weather, which contradicted her melancholy feelings about life and death at the moment.

'Americano please, black with an extra shot.'

The place was buzzing; the downstairs was full of yummy mummies grabbing time with friends between school runs, housework, and probably high-flying careers. Becky tuned in to the nearest table. 'I told Gordon he'd have to wait for the documents until after the school holidays. I said, "I do have a life, you know."' Becky decided her deduction was spot on, but then she *was* a detective.

'Staying in?' the man asked, as he punched at his till.

'What? Sorry, yes. I'll go upstairs.'

'Right, I'll bring it up. That will be three pounds, please.'

Becky paid, and escaped the jolly chatter for the first floor which was still busy, but much quieter.

She found a table by the window. Nearby, two comfortable settees and an armchair were occupied by a group of seven people: two women and five men. One of the women was talking. 'I didn't know if the blood would come off, and my heart started to race.'

Becky stared at her, not quite believing what she was hearing, and then realised with relief that the woman was reading from a notebook, and it wasn't, presumably, some sort of group confession.

Murders Anonymous. Becky smiled at that. She took out her phone and pretended to check it, but she was all ears to know what came next.

'I heard sirens in the distance, and I knew then I would have to run, because nobody was going to believe I hadn't done it!'

The woman looked up from her script and sighed. 'Well,' she asked, 'what do you think? Be honest, now.'

'I like it,' said a man in the group, 'but I think it's moving a bit too fast.'

'Too fast?' said the woman, looking pained. Obviously, she hadn't meant it when she asked for their honesty. 'Two weeks ago you said it was too slow! Make you mind up, Rubin!'

'It's not realistic enough for me,' added another critic. 'You need more blood, more gore, more sex.'

The second woman in the group spoke up. 'We're not all looking for grisly murders you know, David. Some of us happen to like cosy murder mysteries.'

'Rubbish, that isn't real crime,' he spat. 'We're supposed to be a crime writers' group, not the Midsomer Murders fan club.'

Becky was enjoying this little domestic when her coffee arrived. 'Here we go.' The waiter put Becky's cup down and looked over at the now-heated discussion. 'Now guys, what's the problem?' he asked.

'It's just David being a twat again,' said the second woman. Then she smiled, and the tension there a moment before dissolved in laughter.

The group chatted to the waiter, and Becky could tell they all knew each other. 'Anyhow,' asked David, 'how's your bloodbath novel coming along?'

'I've sort of stalled,' said the waiter. 'I'm trying to work out how much blood a body can lose without the victim dying, and how long they'd stay alive for.' The young waiter was medium-sized, with unruly hair that spilled over his eyes.

'Depends on bodyweight and gender.' This came from David, whom Becky had decided was a bit of a know-it-all.

Becky was enjoying this diversion from her real job when her phone rang. 'DC Wainwright,' she answered, on automatic pilot, and then realised that the room had gone very quiet, and every eye was upon her.

6.

In the morgue, Wen stood as far away as she could from the flashing blades and the metal bowls which had bits of human body placed into them at intervals.

John spoke into a mic above his head and his assistant took photos as needed.

At long last it was over, and as the doctor stripped off his gloves and gown, she went to his office for a cup of tea and an unofficial debrief, as was their routine now. Wen made the brews, and the doctor's drink was waiting for him by the time he entered the room.

He sat down and took a long swig of his tea. Then he closed his eyes. 'Bloody hell, I needed that.'

'First findings?' she asked, trying not to sound too pushy.

John didn't say anything for a minute, and he appeared to be thinking. 'She wasn't killed there.'

'But the mess under the body?'

'She was disembowelled there, but not killed. What you saw was fluid from her gut, but she died from asphyxia. A plastic bag was held over her head. There were tiny particles of plastic under her nail beds, and small red marks on her neck where the bag had been twisted tight.'

'Same killer?'

'Nothing to point to that. But I agree with you that the chance of two sadistic killers being in the area at the same time is improbable.'

'Why, thank you for that.' Wen inclined her head and smiled. Good-humoured camaraderie was what kept these two colleagues from going mad at times.

'You're welcome.'

'Time of death?'

'About two days ago. You said there was a dog walker who went into the park at midnight?'

Wen nodded as she sipped her tea. 'He lives nearby, so we got him on the door-to-door.'

'So she was killed and kept somewhere, but cut open after being hung up. I also think you're looking for a physically fit man. It must have taken some strength to pull that girl into that position. And for your man in the bin, as well. Heaving him into one of those big commercial things wouldn't be easy.'

'Or there might have been two of them?'

'It's possible.'

'Any sexual aspects?'

John picked up his cup and finished its contents in one go. 'She hadn't been raped, but a psychologist might say that the very fact she was eviscerated could be seen as a sexual act.'

'Talking of which —'

'You haven't.'

'Not yet, but I think we could do with his input.'

John Baron shook his head slowly. Wen knew there was no love lost between the two men, for various reasons. 'Well, hold off for a little while, because I haven't told you the good news yet.'

'There's good news? Which is?'

'Along with the traces of plastic under her nails, there was something else we've sent for analysis. It might be nothing, but it could be skin from your killer.'

'DNA?'

'Just maybe.'

***

At least now Wen had something to share with the team at the briefing, which was a late one today.

'Right,' she called, to get their attention. 'You all have copies of the latest PM on the female body. We might get a break here, if there is DNA under the victim's nails and we can get a match. Even if we can't do that, we might have some leverage to allow us to take DNA from any suspects. If we ever get any, that is. What have we got on our new lead, Martin Grimes?'

'Nothing yet, boss, I've been busy. I'll get onto it first

thing in the morning,' said Cassie.

'We can exclude one of our missing men, though,' said Jake. 'Paul James returned to his home in Frodsham at lunch-time today.'

'Right.' Wen put a tick against the man's photo. 'And just where had he been? Do we know?'

'Local uniform went to talk to them, and just about managed to stop another murder.'

'Paul wasn't beating up his partner again, was he?' Becky looked at Richard as she said this.

'Not this time. Paul was the one needing protection.' Jake grinned. 'The officers found him being beaten about the head with a very large dildo. Apparently Paul admitted he'd been having an affair for some time, but he wanted to see if it was going to work out before he burnt his bridges.'

'The complete bastard!' said Becky. Then she started laughing. 'At least he got what he deserved, the dickhead.'

'All right you lot, joke over,' said Wen. 'No one in the immediate area has reported a young woman missing, so Jake —'

'Yep. Female missing persons. I'll get on it straight away, boss.'

'The doctor thinks she was about mid to late-twenties. No sign of drug misuse, well-nourished, blonde hair. We're checking dental records, but there's been very little dental work and the fingerprints aren't on file, so once again we have to fill in all the gaps.'

The team started to float away, leaving Wen and Jake alone in the office. Jake was trawling files for a likely missing woman to fit their profile, and Wen was going through the post-mortem reports again. The only thing that the victims had in common, apart from their very brutal murders, was that they had drunk coffee some time before they died. But as clues went, that wasn't even worth worrying about.

7.

The first two had been easy, and his purpose was satisfied. So far.

The police had no idea at all what was going on. There had been little in the press yet; just that two bodies had been found, and that they had died in mysterious circumstances. He knew that very soon they would have to go public with more details, both to stop general speculation and to ask for the public to help with their pathetic enquiries.

He needed more time. Was a week long enough, after all? He would defy their expectations of what a serial killer would do next, break the pattern, and throw any theories they might have into chaos. He also needed time to execute the next one more carefully. He already had a victim in mind, but murdering a police officer would result in the ante being upped significantly. That was exactly what he wanted.

Now it was time for his own press release.

***

It was ten thirty by the time Wen got home. She was shattered and couldn't face going through any more paperwork, even though that was what she had had in mind when she stuffed the files and laptop into her bag.

Wen hung her coat on the banister, noting that her scarf was still in the same place, and realised she would have to deal with Aran's wrath at breakfast tomorrow.

She went to the kitchen and opened the fridge, looking for something to heat up. Her blood sugar was low, and maybe some food and a drink would give her the strength for the background work she hadn't had time for. 'Aran, I love you,' she said when she spied a bowl of stew covered with clingfilm.

With the food heated up, a chunk of bread, and a large glass of white wine, Wen sat down at the kitchen table. Her laptop was open and ready, and she delved into search engines, looking for the weird and not so wonderful.

Two hours later, after she had moved to the more comfortable settee, Wen's eyes drooped. She had been searching for anybody known to the police who'd been investigated for brutal assault and was currently out and about. But no one came anywhere near the type of person they were looking for, and there were some scary people out there.

She would just look at one more thing, then call it a night.

**

'Arwen! Arwen!'

Wen was shaken, less than gently. Her eyes opened slowly, and she wondered for a split second where she was.

'Wake up. You've been asleep on the settee all night.' Aran stood over her like a worried mother ready to scold a naughty child.

'Sorry. I was working late, and I must have dozed off.'

'Well, this won't help.' Aran held the stem of the empty wine glass by the tips of his thumb and forefinger, as if he might catch something from it.

'Aran, I only had one to help me relax.'

Aran, a teetotaler, still looked disgusted. 'And I think we can both conclude that it worked.'

He walked away without another word leaving Wen, yet again, wondering why at thirty-five she still sought her brother's approval. But the thought vanished as the clock on the mantelpiece struck eight and she felt a jolt of adrenaline. 'I'm going to be late!' She headed for the shower, already planning out the day for herself and her team.

Wen was showered, her long blond hair tied back, and in her usual black trouser suit within twenty minutes of being woken by Aran. She noticed that her jacket was rather loose on her; a sure sign that eating was low on her current to-do list, and something she had to watch. She always lost weight when she was on a big case, and at five feet nine she started to look drawn and scrawny very quickly if she wasn't careful.

Back downstairs, she searched for her car keys, then went back to the kitchen for her bag and laptop.

'Aran! What are you doing?' Her brother was poring over her files, while glancing at the computer screen as if he was cross-referencing something. 'How did you get into my laptop?'

'Oh come on, Arwen, it's not hard. Bilbobaggins35. You really need to change your password, and you should look at the security on your software.'

Wen snapped the lid shut. 'That's not the point, Aran.' She collected the files from under his nose and put them in her bag. 'You know damn well that you shouldn't be poking around in my confidential files.' She turned to go before she said anything else.

She had just reached the front door when Aran came into the hall. 'Will you be home for dinner tonight?' he asked.

'No, probably not.' Wen opened the front door and stepped outside.

'You're looking in the wrong places for this murderer. And Arwen...'

Wen looked back at her brother. 'Yes?'

'You still haven't moved your scarf.' Aran turned and went back into the house.

8.

At the same time, in a different part of Warrington, Becky closed her front door. Unlocking her car, she looked up at the 'For Sale' sign and sighed. She loved her house and didn't want to sell it, but had no choice in the matter. Now the divorce was almost final it had to be done. But maybe that was part of the problem; she loved the house more than her soon-to-be-ex-husband.

She would have to start looking seriously at flats, and soon. The house had had a lot of interest, and they'd already had one offer, but as it was new to the market and the offer was a silly one, both herself and Elliot had politely refused it, or as her estranged husband had put it, 'tell them to fuck right off!' The couple who had offered, though, had come for a second viewing, and the estate agent was hopeful they might make a better offer. There had even been talk of surveys. Realistically, Becky knew her lovely home wouldn't be on the market for long, so she needed to work out where she wanted to live, and see what she could afford there.

When she and Elliot had split, her parents suggested she came home to them in London, expecting a broken-hearted daughter to turn up in a state of hysteria. All they got was a phone call saying she was OK, she had a job she loved, and she wasn't about to give all that up because of a broken relationship.

Truthfully, she wasn't heartbroken, more disappointed. Disappointed that she had allowed herself to neglect her marriage, and disappointed that she hadn't been more upset when it had fallen to bits.

But Becky couldn't go back to London. She couldn't return to the disparagement of her mother and father, who still didn't quite believe she had chosen the police instead of putting her law degree to what they considered 'better use', even though a number of chambers had offered her jobs. Becky suspected that was only because her father was a high court judge. And she would never know because she was more than happy with her choice, so her parents would have to get used to the idea that their only child was *just a cop*.

She checked her appearance in her driver's mirror. Her short blond bob could do with a trim soon. She would have to make an appointment with her hairdresser today, because it could be weeks before she might get in.

As Becky reversed off her drive, she decided that the next time she was working in Stockton Heath, she might visit one of the estate agents there. She quite liked the feel of the place. Apart from the dead body strung up in the children's play area at the local park.

***

Down the road, a lone figure watched as Becky left her house. He suspected she lived alone, but he wasn't one hundred per cent sure yet. This would need more surveillance. More patience. He needed to be more calculating with this one. It was hard to hold off, though, after the adrenaline rush the first two kills had given him. It was better than he could have imagined: so much better.

But now he would do his homework. What was the saying? 'Slowly, slowly, catchy monkey'?

Or in this case, a pig!

***

Wen's hand hovered over her phone. She knew that the sooner she got Jeff on board the better it would be for the investigation, and she had her boss's OK, but still she hesitated. She sighed, and let her mind go back to that time when she was happy. Happier than she had ever been. Happier than she had a right to be... Then it had all come tumbling down around her ears, and almost ruined her life.

All because of that man.

'Come on Wen, pull yourself together.' Conscious of the fact John Baron was awaiting some possible DNA results, she could hold off. She probably should hold off, but it was such a long shot that Wen wanted the profiler's input as soon as possible.

She punched in his number, hoping it would go to answerphone; after all, it was Sunday. Then she could leave a voicemail and put off actually speaking to him.

'Hello, Jeff Morgan here... Hello?'

Oh fuck. 'Hello, Jeff. Wen Price here. We'd like your opinion on a case.' Wen felt herself squirm. She hated asking for help, and he'd probably enjoy saying no.

'Hello Wen, how are you? It's so nice to hear from you.' His voice was like warm honey running down the side of a spoon.

'I'm, er, fine, thank you. This case —'

'I did wonder how long it would be before you called me in. Two bodies now, isn't it? Both mutilated?'

'How do you know that? We haven't released that level of detail to the press yet!'

'I've got my contacts, Wen, who keep me in the loop. I'll be over first thing tomorrow. Maybe we can have a catch-up?' And before Wen had a chance to tell Jeff where he could put his 'catch-up', he had ended the call.

This would mean a sleepless night. Wen wondered if she could be civil to the creep face to face.

9.

Today's task for Wen's team was to try and get a handle on where Martin Grimes was, and what his state of mind was like.

Wen and Cassie had made an appointment to see Martin's mother, while Becky and Richard would interview the local mental health team who worked with Martin.

As Wen's car pulled up in front of Mrs Grimes's house in Appleton, Cassie whistled. 'Whoa. That is what I call a house.' The double-fronted Georgian-style property was modern and immaculate.

'This is a million pounds in bricks and mortar,' Cassie continued as she got out of the car. 'Imagine being able to afford something like this.'

'Lovely,' was about all Wen could muster. What people owned had never impressed her, but maybe that was because she had never needed to worry about money.

The front door was open before they had even got half-way along the path. Mrs Grimes was about five feet six inches tall. She was wearing a beautiful baby-blue cashmere dress, and dark bobbed hair framed a small eager face. She wasn't what Cassie had expected at all.

'Welcome, Detectives.' She stood back, allowing them to enter her vast hall. 'Let's go through to the drawing room.' She carefully shut her front door. It was hard to put an accurate age to her, but going by the age of her son she was probably mid to late fifties. 'Can I get you something to drink?'

'No thanks, Mrs Grimes.'

'Laura, please.'

'Laura, we've come to talk to you about Martin. I believe you're worried about him?' asked Wen as she took a seat.

'Of course I'm worried about him. He's my son. He has mental health problems. And he's gone missing.'

'When did you last see him, Laura?' asked Cassie.

'Three days ago. He's gone missing before, of course.'

'Yes, so we believe.' Wen looked at her notes. 'It was two years ago, wasn't it?'

'That's right.' Laura sat neatly on one of the huge settees. 'And two years before that as well. Martin is nothing if not predictable.'

Wen looked at the woman. 'If you don't mind me saying, you don't look that upset.'

Laura pinched her dress into to a pleat. 'I put on a brave face. If I don't, I'll start cracking up as well.'

Cassie took a seat opposite her. 'Does Martin have many friends, Laura?' she asked.

'I don't encourage it,' said Laura.

'Why ever not?' asked Wen.

'It never ends well. He starts to depend on people, and they always let him down eventually. And guess who has to pick up the pieces?'

'Where is Martin's father?' said Cassie.

'Oh, he left years ago. Typical man, couldn't cope when Martin had one of his episodes. Just as well, really. I think if he'd stayed either Martin or I would have killed him by now!'

Cassie and Wen looked up. 'That's rather drastic, Laura,' remarked Wen.

'You wouldn't say that if you'd known him,' Laura replied. 'He had his issues as well, and could be very violent. He often hit me, but he never touched Martin.'

'So what made him leave?' Cassie leaned forward.

'Martin. The day he tried to protect me changed everything.'

'How? In what way?' Wen realised that they were now talking very quietly, almost reverently, to each other.

'The thing about children, officer, is that they grow up. One day Martin got between me and his father. He was just about to stick a knife between Philip's ribs when I stopped him. So Philip had to go, because if he hadn't, then I think Martin would have killed him rather than let him hurt me again.'

'In the past, when Martin has disappeared, where has he turned up?' Cassie asked as she made notes in her book.

'Last time he was found by the police walking along the road in the wrong direction, barefoot and in the pouring rain. The time before, when he set the school on fire, the police picked him up at the scene.'

'And the suicide attempts?'

Laura laughed. 'Suicide attempts! Those weren't suicide attempts, they were — what would you say? A cry for help. My son doesn't want to kill himself; he just wants to make me suffer. And believe me, he is succeeding.'

Cassie and Wen left the house with Martin's toothbrush and a photograph. The toothbrush would give them DNA, and hopefully prove that the male victim now lying in their morgue wasn't Martin Grimes.

***

Becky and Richard sat down in front of the psychiatrist's desk. Dr Sara Nesbitt was sitting opposite, looking at them over her spectacles, her fingers linked together. Becky thought that if she were asked to give a description of a typical psychiatrist, this one would be perfect. Greying hair tied back, nondescript clothes and no makeup. She had a superior look about her, and Becky hoped she was more empathetic with her patients than she appeared to her. But hey, maybe she just didn't like the police.

'So,' said Dr Nesbitt, 'how can I help you?'

'We're here because we believe you have treated Martin Grimes in the past,' said Becky.

'Yes, that's correct. Is Martin in some sort of trouble?'

'What makes you suppose that?' Richard asked.

'Well, I'm presuming you're not here just for a chat.'

'We're actually trying to eliminate him from a serious crime.' Richard's tone was clipped.

'Oh dear. I knew this would happen sooner or later.'

Becky leaned forward, 'You knew what would happen

sooner or later?'

'I knew Martin would do something catastrophic. It wasn't so much if, more when.' She sat back in her seat and looked at the ceiling.

'You think he has the capability to do something that bad?' Richard asked.

'I know he has. He is a very disturbed man.'

'Then why isn't he contained in a facility somewhere, if he's that much of a risk?' Richard couldn't keep the disbelief from his voice.

Dr Nesbitt sighed. 'Because we can't just put people away on a hunch, even if it is backed up by medical knowledge. When Martin set the school on fire he was sectioned for twelve months. He was sectioned again when he harmed himself, but for less time. Once he's settled, and compliant with his medication, we have no reason to keep him in.'

Richard sat back in his seat and folded his arms. 'He has to do something terrible before he can be stopped; is that what you're saying?'

'That's exactly what I'm saying. Just like when *you* know someone has broken the law, but you can't prove it.' Dr Nesbitt folded her own arms as if to say *game, set and match*.

Richard strode away from the clinic, shoulders rigid, then wrenched the car door open, dropped into the driver's seat, and slammed the door with a bang.

'Want me to drive?' Becky asked.

'No. Why would I want you to drive?'

'Because you're in a bad mood.'

'I'm not in a bad mood,' Richard barked. He backed out of his parking space sharply, then stopped as metal crunched on metal. 'Oh fuck!' Richard hit the steering wheel and watched the angry driver behind him grow larger in his wing mirror as he walked towards them.

10

'You did what?'

'It's just a scratch, ma'am. He pulled up behind me and I didn't see him.'

'You didn't bloody look, you mean. It's not the scrape, Richard, it's all the paperwork involved. I just don't need this now.' Wen sighed. 'I suppose I should be grateful that nobody was hurt.'

'Yes ma'am.'

'OK, don't do it again.' Wen shook her head. 'God, I sound like your mother telling you off for smoking out of your bedroom window. Did you actually get anything from the psychiatrist?'

'Only that this Martin Grimes is a bit of a psychopath. According to her, there's nothing they can do until he does something really serious.' Richard grimaced.

Wen raised her eyebrows. 'Burning down a school isn't serious anymore?'

'Ah well, you see, because he was off his meds he can't be held responsible. Even though he was sectioned for a year. Dr Nesbitt said that when he's on his medication he's a fully functioning member of society.' Richard did air quotes with his fingers.

'Well thank the Lord for that, then.' Wen looked at the whiteboard. There was plenty of writing, but not much information to go forward with. 'So, what next?'

'Well, we've still got to go and see the unit where Martin was held,' said Becky. 'We're going to talk to one of the nurses and see what he was like when he was there.'

'Good, maybe we'll get a handle on him that way. What about forensics? Any joy there?'

'The DNA doesn't match the Polish lad,' said one of the officers from the back of the room.

'That's good. I don't suppose he's turned up yet?' asked Wen.

'No sign of him, ma'am. I could go and see the girlfriend again,' Cassie suggested.

'No, we can't be chasing after him just because he's gone off somewhere. We know he's not the body, so we'll leave that with missing persons.' Wen turned to look at the board again. 'We're not much further forward really, and now we've got a dead female as well. There might be some DNA evidence there, but we'll have to wait a few days.' She looked at Jake. 'Any interesting females gone missing recently?'

For once, Jake looked down in the mouth. 'Sorry ma'am, nothing local that fits our victim.'

'Right, then you'll have to cast your net further afield.'

Jake sighed. 'Yes ma'am, but you know that could throw up maybe twenty or thirty people to look at?'

'Do you know what, Jake, I did actually know that,' said Wen, sarcasm dripping from her words. 'We have to start looking wider. The body might not be from anywhere near here, but we've got to start somewhere.'

Wen gave the team different tasks to be going on with: phone calls, door-knocking, internet searches. 'And just so you know,' she said, 'I'm getting a profiler involved. He's coming tomorrow to give us his opinion, and I need your full co-operation. Cassie, you can work with him for the day.' Wen had already decided she wasn't going to be the one going head to head with Jeff.

'Oh, and finally, we're doing a press release later,' she said. 'We'll give out more information, and appeal for the public's help.'

'Ma'am, I think you might want to see this,' said Jake.

'What?' Wen asked as she approached Jake's desk and looked over his shoulder at the screen. Her mouth dropped open as she read: 'HORRIFIC MURDERS KEPT QUIET BY POLICE'. It was the headline on a national paper. Worse, there were photos. Even though they were pixelated, they suggested grisly findings.

'Who the fuck has leaked this?' she asked.

No one spoke. The silence stretched longer, and longer.

***

'What the hell happened here?'

Charles Manning paced behind his desk, which showed his agitation. Wen had never seen him so ruffled.

'I've spoken to comms, sir, and their best guess is that a member of the public has taken the photos and gone to the press. They aren't crime scene photos, sir.'

Charles stared at her. 'What has the newspaper got to say?'

'Not a lot. They're screaming about their right to print the truth, and asking why we haven't been honest with the public.' Wen stood to attention, feeling the knots in her shoulders.

Charles sat down and sighed. 'We can't keep anything quiet these days because of bloody social media! It would have come out soon, but I wanted us to manage the press, not the other way round!'

'Yes, sir. Comms have rewritten the press statement in the light of what's already been printed.'

'Yes, I've seen it.' He looked past her absentmindedly. 'Are you OK to front that?'

'Yes, sir.'

'I'll sit in on it, of course.'

'Of course, sir.'

'All right, DI Price. Have we got anything to take to this press release, apart from the psychobabble comms gave us? It's like being a politician these days. We don't answer questions, we just circumnavigate them.'

'We're looking into how such good photos were taken, sir.'

'Why? What do you mean?' For the first time, the chief inspector made eye contact with Wen.

'We had the area sealed off very quickly, and those photos weren't taken with someone's phone. They were shot using a zoom lens. And the angle is wrong for anyone in the SOCO to have taken them.'

'What's your thinking, Wen?'

'Either someone with a good camera saw this when we did, and took the photos to sell them to a paper, or —'

'Or the killer took them!'

'Could be, sir.'

11.

'Come with me, Cassie,' said Wen. 'We're off to Media City to talk to the editor of *that* newspaper.' Cassie grabbed her bag and coat in one swift action. 'Becky and Richard, go back to Stockton Heath and see if you can pin down the area where those photos were taken. Take a camera with a zoom lens with you, for perspective. The rest of you, get on with your jobs.' With that, Wen and Cassie were gone.

Becky looked at Richard, then raised her eyes to heaven. 'As if we wouldn't have thought to take a camera with us, for God's sake. I like the DI, but sometimes she treats us like we're still wet behind the ears.'

'Just crossing the Ts and dotting the Is, you know what's she's like. You get the camera, I'll get the car and meet you outside in ten. If you're lucky, when we've finished, I'll buy you a coffee in one of those posh coffee shops on the high street.'

'No expense spared, eh?' Becky smiled and then punched Richard's arm.

'Ouch! Just get the camera, Becky. See you in ten.'

Becky stuck out her tongue at her partner and switched on the printer so that they could take copies of the photos to the crime scene with them. As the machine spat out the necessary information, she went in search of the office camera.

When they reached the park it was raining; dull sleeting rain trying hard to be snow. Becky shivered as she walked from the climbing frame to the most logical spot for the photos to be taken from. Richard was in front, his long legs leaving her short ones behind as he strode out to the distance estimated by one of the techies as their starting point.

Richard turned his collar up against the rain as he disappeared behind a group of trees at the edge of the park. Looking back, he saw Becky jogging towards him, head down. She was tiny compared with him, and they had the nickname of Little and Large back at the station. Pity he was married. He could go for Becky in a big way, especially now her excuse for a husband was off the scene. They worked well together, covered each other's backs, he trusted her...

'What do you think?' she asked as she caught up with him.

'What?'

'The photos.' She shivered. 'From here, do you think?'

Richard took the camera out of its leather bag and attached the lens. 'Let's see.' He pressed a button and moved the camera in a small, slow arc. 'Let me see those photos again.'

Becky took the printed sheets from her bag and they both looked at the images. 'Further back, I think. But it depends how good the person's lens was.'

They moved back a few more metres and Richard looked through the viewfinder. 'That's about it. Tell me what you think.' He passed the piece of equipment carefully to Becky. 'God, these things are heavy. Give me my good old phone camera any day.'

'It's more the lens that's heavy.' Becky looked at the scene through the camera. 'Yes, I think you're right. Around here, at any rate. I'll just take a few shots to show the boss when we get back.' But when she looked up, she found she was talking to herself.

Richard had walked a few feet away. 'Becks...'

'Just a mo. One more —'

'Becky, *now!*'

'What?' Becky turned to see Richard crouched down, staring at something on the ground. 'What have you found?' She approached tentatively, and as she drew level she could see over Richard's shoulder. 'Is — is that blood?'

Richard nodded.

Becky pulled out her phone and stabbed at it with her finger. 'Hello, DC Rebecca Wainwright speaking. Can you put me through to the forensic unit, please?'

***

'Can I see the person in charge?' Wen stood in the reception of the *Daily Comment*, full of glass and shining chrome.

'I'm sorry, do you have an appointment?' asked the Barbie doll behind the desk, her big, bright smile making Wen wish she had her sunglasses on.

'No, but —'

'Let me stop you there. Mr Blackmore is a very busy man, and —'

'Let me stop *you* there.' Wen and Cassie both produced their IDs, which left Barbie girl looking dazed and confused. 'Now, please! Mr Blackmore isn't the only one who's busy.'

The receptionist grabbed at the phone and pressed something. 'Mr Blackmore, sorry to bother you, sir. Yes, I know you said you weren't to be disturbed, but… Yes sir, I know that, but —'

Wen snatched the receiver from the receptionist's hand. 'Mr Blackmore. DI Price here from Cheshire Serious Crime Squad. I need to see you immediately.' Wen listened for a few seconds. 'Thank you.'

She handed the phone back to the receptionist. 'Tell us where to find him, please.'

Five minutes later they were in the office of the editor of one of the biggest daily papers in the country. William Blackmore was a larger-than-life figure, sitting behind a big desk in his smart three-piece suit. That, with his designer stubble and careful hairstyle, gave him an air of self-importance which left Wen cold.

'So, ladies, how can I help you?' He smiled a smile that didn't reach his eyes.

'The story you ran this morning?'

'Yes, and I've already told you we cannot divulge our sources. I'm surprised you've come all this way, to be honest. We've already had this conversation with your press guy,' he said, tapping a pen on the edge of the desk.

Wen was tempted to grab it from him and poke him in the eye, but resisted. Instead she smiled her best smile. 'I realise this, Mr Blackmore, and I respect your right to protect your source. However —'

'There isn't a however, Inspector —'

'However, this, as you saw from the photos, is a truly horrific crime, and we suspect that the person who took those photos may be the killer.'

William Blackmore sat up straight. 'Really?' He looked far too pleased for comfort. This wasn't going the way Wen wanted. No wonder the police employed experienced ex-journalists to deal with the vultures they used to be.

'We need to know how you came by those photos. I'd bet my pension that no names were given.'

The editor leaned back in his chair. 'What's in this for the paper if we cooperate?'

'My undying gratitude.' Wen smiled. Blackmore smiled back, shaking his head. 'No? Well, how about this press release, before anyone else gets it?'

Blackmore put his hand out for the paper Wen had produced from her bag, but she moved it out of his reach. 'Is that all?' he said.

'And we'll give you an exclusive about the case before the other papers get a sniff, if you do the same for us.'

'We received the photos by email, with the subject line: *The public deserve to know the details*. That's it.'

'Right.' Wen handed him the press release. 'I'll send one of our IT guys round to see if he can locate where the email was sent from.'

'That's not very convenient for the office,' Blackmore complained, as he scanned the press release Wen had just handed to him.

'It's either that, or we get a warrant and take the computer back to HQ with us. Entirely up to you.'

He nodded.

'I'm glad we see eye to eye on this matter,' said Wen. 'Now I'd like a copy of those photos without the pixelation, please. And the email.'

He pressed an intercom. 'Penny, can you print out a copy of the email we received on the cover story.'

'Thank you. We'll let you get back to your work now, Mr Blackmore.' Wen and Cassie stood to go.

Mr Blackmore looked at Cassie. 'Can't you talk?'

Cassie stared at him, not bothering to reply.

'I've noticed that women seem to be taking over the police force,' said the editor, settling back in his seat.

Wen looked at him. 'Maybe that's because we're good at what we do.'

'Maybe,' he replied, in a way that made it clear he didn't believe it. 'But why do they send you in pairs? Is it like the toilet thing where you have to go together?'

'Prick,' said Cassie very quietly as she left the room, but she knew he had heard her.

12.

'Nice coffee.'

Becky and Richard were sitting upstairs in an otherwise empty 24/7, trying to get warm. Becky nursed her cup, hoping her fingers would thaw out soon. Richard had drained his first coffee and was now sipping the second more slowly. Their quick scouting mission to find the site the photos were taken from had turned into a marathon lasting five long, cold hours.

SOCO had done a meticulous search of the area where the blood had been found, taking many samples for inspection, and possibly testing. 'Of course, this might be animal blood,' said the scene manager. 'Or it might not relate to the crime at all.'

'Give us a break, Norman,' said Richard. 'How likely is it that blood in the same area that the photos were taken isn't connected with that girl's body?' He waved the photos in his hand in the man's face.

'I just don't want you to get your hopes up, that's all.'

Now caffeinated, and slightly warmer, Becky and Richard tried to rationalise what they had found.

'He's right, of course,' said Becky.

'Who?'

'Keep up, Richard. Norman. It might be a dog with a bleeding paw, or someone who had a nosebleed.'

'And ran into the woods? Yeah, right. Mark my words, that's either our victim's blood or the perp's.'

Becky nodded and finished her coffee. Just at that moment the jolly waiter came upstairs and began to wipe tables and collect cups. He smiled at Becky, then came over to their table. 'Hi, would you like another one?'

'No, I'm good thanks,' said Becky.

He moved away, then turned back. 'I know you, you're that detective. You came in the day they found that poor lass in the park.'

'Yes, the day of the writing thingy.' She waved her arm towards the area where the group had been sitting.

'Our crime writing club. Yes, that's right.' He sat down on one of the empty chairs next to Richard. 'We all wanted to pick your brains, but you disappeared.'

'Oh yes. I got a call and I had to leave.'

'Crime writing, you say?' asked Richard, with an eager look on his face.

'Yes. It's loads of fun. Do you fancy joining us? You'd be more than welcome. A real life detective on the team! That would be a dream come true.'

'Do you write, Richard?' Becky asked incredulously.

Richard stretched his legs out under the table. 'Well, I have been known to knock out the odd bit of prose.'

'Really?' Becky began to wonder what else she didn't know about her colleague.

'Fancy writing a crime novel?' asked the waiter.

'Maybe.' Richard smiled to himself. 'It could be a nice little sideline.'

'Seriously?' Becky squeaked. Richard looked over, but he was saved by the bell of her phone. 'Yes boss. We're on our way back now. Yep, see you soon.' She looked at her partner. 'Got to go.'

Richard drained the rest of his coffee and handed his cup to the waiter. 'Thanks...'

'Just call me Dante.'

'OK. See you.'

'Don't be a stranger.'

As they headed back to the car Becky looked at Richard, who had a secret little smile on his face. 'I think "Just call me Dante" might be your first fan.' She dug him in the ribs.

'Do one, Becky,' he replied, but the smile didn't go away.

***

'We're moving forward. Slowly, mind you, but at last we have some leads.'

Wen sat on the edge of one of the desks in the large office, her officers straggling around her as they did a round-up of the day's findings before going home.

'We have an area in the trees near the second murder scene where we suspect the photos were taken, and Richard found blood traces there.' She nodded at Richard to take up the narrative.

'SOCO have taken various samples, but it's the blood that could be the biggest lead.' He paused. 'It might just be the murderer's own blood.'

'What makes you think that?' asked Cassie. A couple of her colleagues rolled their eyes, but she ignored them. She didn't question things to annoy people, it was how her mind worked.

'Well, we didn't see any blood when we were walking away from the scene, so it's a good bet it's not the victim's.'

'We can but hope,' Wen said quietly.

'Even if it is the perpetrator's blood,' said Cassie, 'he might not be in our system.'

'Thanks, Sarge.' Richard clenched his hands, trying to control his frustration.

'Just saying, that's all,' said Cassie, holding her hands up in conciliation.

'But what we do know,' said Wen, 'or what we're ninety-nine per cent sure of, is that the killer took the photos and then sent then to the *Daily Comment*. If we can get an IP address, we might have the bastard.'

Wen got up, went over to the whiteboard, and stood, considering the information, before turning back to her team. 'Right, tomorrow. I'm speaking to the media with the chief inspector at ten. Cassie, you're with our profiler all day. Becky and Richard, organise a house-to-house around Stockton Heath again with the tidied-up photo of the girl's face. Oh yes, and while you're in the area go around local cafes and restaurants, I believe there are quite a few. See if anyone recognises her. Was she a customer, did she work for any of them? Pop in the shops and ask there as well.'

'Yes ma'am,' Becky and Richard responded together.

'And when are you visiting the unit Martin Grimes was an inpatient at?'

'The day after tomorrow, ma'am,' Richard replied. 'The nurse we need to speak to isn't on until then. Unless you want us to go to his house tomorrow?'

'No, Thursday will do. I think it would be better to see the place as well, see how it runs.'

'And we might get some more DNA results tomorrow,' added Cassie.

'Yep. So, off home now, and we'll have another team meeting this time tomorrow. In the meantime, feed any information back to Jake.' Wen looked around. 'Where is Jake?'

'Hospital appointment, ma'am. He did ask.'

'Is that today? Right, see you all tomorrow, then.'

The bodies drifted away, muttering to each other, complaining about the long hours, the lack of real progress and their colleagues. All quite normal.

Wen sighed. It had been a long day, and she was tired. Time to go home, say hi to her brother, and try and get some sleep. She wasn't looking forward to tomorrow. Not so much the press conference, even though she hated them; speaking in public had never been her forte. No, it wasn't that. It was the fact that Jeff was going to be here. She would try and keep out of his way for as long as possible. However, being the SIO, at some point she'd have to talk to him.

She wondered if Jeff had changed; she doubted it. He was probably the same sanctimonious twat he had always been. It was so annoying that she needed to call him at all. But when all was said and done, he was the best at what he did. Wen couldn't let her pride hinder the progress of the case. She couldn't risk putting more people in danger just because she couldn't stand that man.

Wen was sure things would look better tomorrow, after a good night's sleep. As things stood at the moment, they probably couldn't look any worse.

13.

Aran tutted as Wen flopped down on the settee in the kitchen. 'You look wrong,' he said as he put the kettle on.

'Gee thanks, bro.' Wen knew what he was saying. Even if Aran sometimes couldn't grasp the right words, she always knew what he meant. 'I'm tired. It's been a long day.'

'Twenty-four hours. No day is longer than any other. Well apart from a few minutes here and there that is.'

'Yes, but it seemed much longer.'

'Are you getting anywhere?'

'Not really. Lots of leads, all going nowhere.'

'Would you like some lentil soup?' Aran said as he made a pot of tea.

'I'd like steak and chips.'

'Fine. As long as you cook it yourself. I've made lentil soup.'

'Sorry, Aran. Sounds wonderful.' Wen felt slightly guilty when she complained about the food her brother served up. It was always delicious, and he put a lot of time and effort into his meals, even if it wasn't always what she would have cooked for herself. Aran didn't ever ask what she would like. You got what he had cooked. End of!

Wen stretched, then put her head back against the settee and closed her eyes. She felt as if she were falling into a big black hole, and the lack of evidence was sucking her into a vacuum. She couldn't breathe, she couldn't move, and the only thing she could see was Jeff grinning at her. She wanted to scream at him, 'This is your fault. You ruined my future. You said you loved me!'

'Wen. Wen! Wake up.'

Wen opened her eyes and tried to focus on her brother's face, but it was blurred. Then she realised she was crying. She sat up and tried to wipe away the tears running down her face.

'Soup's ready.' Aran sat down at the kitchen table and started eating his meal. Wen dragged herself onto her feet and sat opposite him, feeling as if she had been in a boxing match.

'Why are you upset?' Aran asked, as he pulled a big chunk of bread from the fresh loaf in the middle of the table.

'I'm not. Pass the bread, please.'

Aran pushed the bread basket towards his sister. 'Yes you are. Is it this case?'

'No. Well, kind of, in a roundabout sort of way.' She popped some bread into her mouth.

'What sort of way?'

Wen sighed. 'Jeff Morgan is coming to the office tomorrow.'

'Oh!'

'Oh, indeed.'

The silence that followed fizzed with unspoken tension as they ate their meal.

Aran looked at her. 'Do you have —'

'Yes, Aran, I have to. Believe me, if there was another profiler I could ask, I would.'

'After what he did to you?'

'That was years ago.' Wen tried to sound matter of fact, as if she didn't care.

'But he still has the power to make you cry.'

Wen got up to rinse her bowl and put it in the dishwasher. She looked at her brother. 'Aran?'

'Yes?'

'When you said we were looking for the killer in the wrong place, what did you mean?'

'You were looking at people with some sort of criminal record.'

'Yes, so?'

'This is a new killer. Well, of humans, that is. He's trying to prove something.'

'Prove something? To whom, and why?'

Aran shrugged. 'I'm not sure. You — that is the police —

or maybe himself.'

'And how did you come up with this fascinating theory?'

Aran closed his eyes and thought. 'It's something I've read, but I'm not sure where or when.' He opened his eyes again and shook his head. 'It will come to me. If I didn't have to take those tablets I wouldn't have this problem. You know that, don't you?'

'You have to take them, Aran. Promise me you won't stop.'

'Of course I won't. Even if they do make my mind dull, and I hate the way they make me feel.'

'Yes, but they are important. Don't ever just stop taking them.'

Aran gave her a look, put his bowl in the dishwasher, and walked away without another word.

***

Becky closed her front door and kicked off her shoes. She headed straight for the kitchen and extracted a bottle of wine from the fridge. Pouring herself a large glass, she gave thanks that most bottles these days had screw tops, and you didn't have to play tug of war with a cork anymore. When she was tired and frustrated that never ended well.

Padding into the lounge, Becky flopped in her favourite chair, reached for the TV remote, and channel-surfed for something that might hold her concentration for more than a nanosecond. She didn't really like television, but when she was in the middle of a case her mind roamed all over the place, especially at night, and it usually took a couple of glasses of wine to get her to sleep. The TV acted as a distraction, when she could find anything worth watching.

Before Elliot had left, she used him as a sounding board, confident she could tell him anything under the sun and it would never go any further. She never went into detail, but he was a good listener. That side of their relationship she did miss.

Becky put her glass on the coffee table as her phone vibrated to tell her a text had just landed.

It was Richard. 'Pauline wants to know if you want to come around for supper?'

'No thanks partner. Just downed first glass of wine. See you tomorrow. Say thanks to Pauline,' she replied.

Becky smiled. Richard was good to work with, and they got on really well. In fact, Elliot had asked her outright whether she was having an affair with Richard when she told him that their marriage was over.

Richard was a one-woman man, and he and Pauline were solid. Otherwise, her answer might have been different.

Becky decided to have a shower and get into her PJs, make herself beans on toast, and have another glass of wine so she could fall asleep in front of the telly. She dragged herself upstairs to her bedroom.

As she approached the doorway she stopped. Something felt odd, as if someone were watching her. She tiptoed into her room, then the en suite. No, nothing. 'Get a grip,' she told herself as she slipped off her clothes and ran the shower. Under the warm stinging jets of water, she felt the stress of the day roll away.

Eyes shut, she reached for her shampoo. It wasn't there. But she always left it in exactly the same place, always! And if that shampoo wasn't where it had been this morning, someone had moved it.

14.

'Have you any idea who is committing these horrific crimes, Detective Inspector?'

The question came from a journalist at the front of the room, which was filled to capacity. Some news channels, every paper in circulation, and some that weren't. All you needed was a press card to gain entrance, and there seemed to be an abundance of those this morning.

'We are following up some significant leads,' said Wen, 'and we are appealing to the public for help in this case. If anyone thinks that either of the victims are known to them, or if they saw anything that might be of interest to us, we ask them to please call us on this number.' Wen turned, and pointed to the phone number emblazoned above them. 'All calls will be treated in the strictest confidence, of course.'

'So you haven't got a clue who the killer is, then?' This came from a disembodied voice at the back.

The chief inspector leaned forward. 'As DI Price has said, we are following various leads, and also waiting on forensic results to enable us to narrow our search.' Their united front should discourage the baying press hounds who wanted to tear this meeting to bits.

'Are you looking at any "persons of interest" at the moment?' This came from a female reporter, Jan Redford. Wen had crossed swords with Jan in the past; she tried to undermine their work at every opportunity.

'No, Ms Redford, at this moment in time we are not looking at any particular individual.'

'Should the general public be concerned? After all, we have a potential Jack the Ripper on the loose.'

'No, they should go about their normal activities. I would advise people not to go into dark lonely areas on their own, but then that's never advisable. And please, Jan, do *not* use such inflammatory titles for these cases.'

'Why not, Detective Inspector?' Jan asked, smiling.

'Because you don't know what you're talking about, that's why,' Wen snapped.

'Thank you, that will be all for now,' said Charles Manning. He and Wen got up to leave, questions still being hurled at them from every part of the room.

'God, that was awful.' Wen felt herself shaking as they walked away from the meeting room and back to the guts of the police station.

'You did well. They're like vultures circling a dead animal. It doesn't matter who gets hurt, as long as they get their story.'

'Yes, but we need them on our side. I know asking the public for help means a ton more work for us, but there just might be someone out there who knows one of the victims. They've got to have mothers, fathers, family. People that love them, and miss them. Haven't they?'

'You would hope so,' the chief inspector replied. 'Our problem is if they are immigrants, especially if they're here illegally.'

With that thought pinging around in her head, Wen decided to get some fresh air before the next attack on her overloaded brain.

***

'Nice to meet you, Detective Sergeant.' Jeff Morgan took Cassie's hand and gave it a warm, gentle shake, while at the same time unleashing his full-on sexy smile. At least, that was how he perceived their introduction.

Cassie smiled back. 'Pleased to meet you, Dr Morgan. I've heard a lot about you.'

There was a sentence that held many meanings. 'All good, I hope?'

'Of course. I studied one of your modules when I did my degree. "The autistic mind: responsible or not". It was very interesting.'

Jeff leaned closer, taking in Cassie's heady perfume. She was very attractive. Lean body, long legs, nice skin. 'Glad I could be of service.'

Cassie moved back slightly, then turned away. 'I have copies of the case files for you, Dr Morgan, and the DI said you would probably want to visit the scenes?'

'Call me Jeff, please, and yes, Wen knows me so well. Where is she, by the way?'

'Press conference. She's sorry she couldn't be here to see you herself, but you have me at your disposal all day.' Cassie was now behind her desk, having very gradually put more space between herself and the good doctor.

'Pity. But I'm sure I'll get a chance for a catch-up at some point today. And I'm grateful she thinks I'm worth the time of her second in command. Now then, Cassie — it is Cassie, isn't it?' Cassie nodded. 'Just point me towards a quiet corner where I can have a look at this lot, and then we can go and see where the bodies were found.'

Cassie showed Jeff into an interview room and, after providing him with a coffee, left him to it. When she had been asked by Wen to work with Jeff, Cassie had jumped at the chance to spend a day with the renowned Dr Morgan, criminal psychologist and profiler. Now she had met him, Cassie wasn't sure whether she had been handed a poisoned chalice.

∗∗∗

Becky felt she was on a hamster wheel, asking the same questions and getting the same answers, but that was what ninety per cent of police work was about. Going over and over the same information with different people, trying to engage with them, encouraging them to think, making the questions seem important, making *them* feel important, hoping for just a spark of something that might bring them closer to the truth.

Richard had taken one side of the high street in Stockton Heath, and she had taken the other side, agreeing to meet at 24/7 when they had finished. One more business to go, and then that much-needed drink was hers. Becky was becoming quite a regular client at that coffee emporium, but it had quiet nooks where she and Richard could go over their notes without being heard, and the coffee was good.

The next business was an estate agent, and Becky found herself gazing into the window for any flats that might take her fancy. And there it was. Just come onto the market, according to the information in the window. On the edge of the village, in a converted brewery building, offering luxury accommodation with easy access to all motorway routes, etc., etc.

'It's lovely, isn't it?'

Becky jumped. She had been so enthralled by the idea of that property that she hadn't heard anyone come up behind her. She turned to see a well-dressed man, probably in his early forties, smiling at her. 'Sorry?' She swallowed hard, her heart thumping in her chest.

'Oh, I'm so sorry.' The man stepped back. 'I startled you.'

'You did a bit,' Becky said, as she started to regain her poise. The man wore a smart suit. He had a tray of take-out coffees in one hand and a bag from the local patisserie in the other.

'I'm David Lowery.' Becky looked enquiringly at him. Should that mean something to her? 'Lowery and Bancroft Estate Agents?' Still nothing. He looked upwards.

Becky followed his gaze. There, above their heads, was the man's name in huge letters. 'Oh! *That* David Lowery.'

'Coffee run.' He held up the bag. 'Come in, and I'll sort the details of the flat out for you.'

Becky found herself opening the door for the man, then following him into the office. 'No. That is, that's not really why I'm here.' Then quietly, to herself, 'I might as well have a look.'

'Coffee's up, girls.' David Lowery put his purchases down on the nearest table, to much positive comment. 'I'll just get you the details of that flat. Little beauty. Won't be on the market long. Would you like to arrange a viewing?'

'I'm not actually here about property, Mr Lowery, though I do need to start looking soon.' She produced her warrant card. 'DC Wainwright, Cheshire Serious Crime Squad.'

'Right. Sorry, I thought...' He looked at the brochure he had in his hand.

Becky noticed that the chatter in the room had evaporated, and silence floated around them like an unwelcome ghost. 'Have you seen this woman before?' She produced the photo.

David Lowery took the photo from her and gave it all his attention. 'I don't think so, though she does look familiar. But then we see so many people in here.' He passed it to his colleagues. 'Have any of you seen this lady?'

The women passed it around, all shaking their heads, and Becky took the time to study the estate agent more carefully. 'I've seen you before somewhere.'

'Well, my face is in the local paper every week, so maybe —'

'No, I know where. 24/7. You're one of the crime writers.'

'Yes, that's right, and you were having a coffee. Yes, I remember now.'

It was another blank. No one at the estate agents had seen the woman, but they were quite happy to put her photo in their window, as were all the other shops and business Becky had called on.

'Well, thank you for that.' Becky made some notes in her pocketbook and turned to leave.

'You're forgetting something.' David Lowery handed her the details on the flat. 'You said you needed to start looking.'

'Yes, but —'

'Just read the information pack, then give me a call if you want to view it. No harm in having a peek.'

Becky smiled. 'You're good at your job, Mr Lowery. Thanks, I'll consider it.'

'As I'm sure you are at yours, DC Wainwright. Call me.'

***

'Did you get anywhere?' Becky asked Richard as she rested her feet on the seat opposite. She had put her bag on the chair, and didn't feel too bad about her flagrant breach of etiquette.

'Not a sniff. All very concerned and helpful, but no one knows her. Or if they do, they're not letting on. You?'

'Same.'

'A complete waste of time, then!' Richard shut his pocketbook and threw his pen down with a clatter.

'Not a complete waste of time. I've found a flat.'

'Well, good for you.' Becky looked over her cup at Richard and saw the frustration on his face, but she couldn't help smiling.

'What?' Richard asked.

'You. You always do this.'

'Do what?'

'Let the job get to you.'

Richard frowned at her. 'Bloody hell, Becky, people are being hacked to death out there. Don't you care?'

'Of course I care. But you let it get to you. Carry on like this and you'll be a basket case by the time you're thirty.'

Richard smiled, and visibly relaxed. He knew she was right; that was why they made such a good team. He was emotional, involved and complicated in his thinking. She was logical, distant and systematic in her working life. They were yin and yang, and for the most part they balanced each other out.

'Back to base, then. Let's see if anyone else has done better than we have,' Richard said as he drained his cup.

15.

Jeff stood for a long time, looking at the climbing frame. He didn't say anything, just stood there, staring. Cassie wasn't sure if she should break the silence, but decided against it. She was just beginning to wonder whether he would notice if she walked away when he looked at her. 'Strange,' he said.

'Is it? I lean more towards weird, and not in a good way.'

'But why here? I mean, the bin was a clumsy attempt at hiding the body, but here...?'

'Do you think it might be the same killer?' Cassie followed Jeff as he hurried towards their car.

'Definitely. But here it's as if he wanted to say, "This is me, look at what I'm capable of."'

Jeff stopped abruptly, and Cassie bumped into him. He turned, and looked at the murder site again. 'Right, let's get back. I want to make some notes before I brief your boss.'

***

Back at the office Wen found most of her team, plus a few dozen extra staff, all busy answering phone calls, looking at computer screens, or making notes. As expected, the call for the public's help had generated vast amounts of laborious work. All calls had to be logged, looked at, and if necessary followed up.

Some of the stranger calls might include someone having seen an alien from outer space with blood dripping from its jaws, or a tip that the culprit was a wild animal that had escaped from a zoo some forty miles away. Those tipoffs were usually put in what the team called 'the loony bin'. That file, labelled 'extreme information,' was seldom consulted, and it had its own 'frequent flyers'; the same names ringing in with wild stories each time a serious crime was committed. Wen had spent a few hours going through the file once. At first she had found it amusing, but after a while she had decided that the human race was doomed, and this was the proof.

'Let's have a team meeting in thirty minutes, please,' said Wen. 'All calls to go to the answer service, though I do want real people on the other end of those lines for the next twenty-four hours at least.'

A few sighs and exasperated looks made Wen feel very demanding, but that emotion was soon replaced by grim determination to get this murderer before he struck again.

Thirty minutes later the space was quiet, with an undercurrent of whispers as Wen turned to the room. 'Door to door, anything there?'

Richard spoke up for his team. 'Not a sausage, ma'am. Lots of people took posters, but not one person recognised the girl in the photo.'

'Right. Anything helpful come through on the calls?' She put this to a young female uniformed officer who had been put in charge of the phone lines, with strict instructions to pass anything of interest to one of Wen's detectives.

'A few things that I've passed onto Jake,' she said with confidence, 'but all calls have been logged. When things slow down, I'll take another closer look at everything, ma'am.'

'Thank you, constable. And what did get passed your way, Jake?'

'A couple of reported sightings around the time of the murder, and a few people saying they know who the victim is. All being followed up as we speak, ma'am.'

'Good. Keep me informed, Jake, please. Now, nothing else yet on forensics, but I'll —'

Jeff burst into the room, quickly followed by Cassie. He stopped, caught Wen's eye, and smiled straight at her. Wen wanted to run and hide in her office. Her hands were damp and her mouth was dry, but she managed to hold her ground.

Jeff took off his jacket and tossed it over a chair. 'Ah, we've just come at the right time, I think.' His eyes never left her face; Wen was sure she had gone bright red.

'Dr Jeff Morgan, everyone,' she said, finally managing to

pull her gaze away from his. 'Dr Morgan is here to help us with a possible profile of our killer. Presuming it is just the one killer, that is?'

'Oh yes, I think we are safe with that conclusion.' He advanced and stood next to Wen, far too close for her comfort.

'Over to you then, Dr Morgan.' Wen moved to one side and sat down before her legs gave way. She hadn't expected seeing him again to have this dramatic effect on her.

'I've read the case notes and visited the crime scene, and I will have to sit down and analyse this more deeply, but I concur with your DI.' Jeff surveyed his audience. 'This is the same perpetrator, and he will kill again soon!'

16.

'How are you, Wen?' Jeff followed her into her office as the crew started to break up and return to their business.

Wen scuttled behind her desk and sat down. She started shuffling papers around, to catch her breath and also work out a way to cope with her present antagonist. 'I'm just fine, thank you. When can I expect your full report?' She had a feeling Jeff was not fooled for one moment.

'Tomorrow afternoon.' He sat on the edge of her desk, getting as close as he could to her. 'I've got a lecture in the morning, but I'll get on to it as soon as I can after that.'

'Close of play tomorrow, then?'

'If not before. Wen, can we go for a drink, or a coffee maybe?'

'We have a very good coffee machine in the office. Help yourself.' Wen turned to her computer screen and put her warrant card into it to boot it into life.

'That's not what I meant, and you know it.'

'Do I?' Wen managed to look at Jeff. 'We went beyond cups of coffee and nice chats a long time ago. Now if you don't mind, I've got a lot of work to do.'

Jeff stood up and sighed. 'After all these years, you still hold a grudge? It's not healthy, you know. I thought you might have had the good grace to forgive me by now.'

Wen stood too, rage coursing through her. 'Forgive you? Are you serious? You almost ruined my life, and Aran has become a recluse because of what you wrote.'

'You can't blame me for that. Given his history, I suspect that withdrawal from society would have happened anyway.'

'Just get out, Jeff, now!'

He gave her one last look, shook his head sadly, then left. Wen sank back into her chair and realised she was trembling. After all these years he still had power over her, and she didn't like it one bit.

**

Richard had driven Becky back to her house and now they sat outside, going over the end-of-shift meeting. 'I think there's history between those two,' Richard said, wanting to see if his partner thought the same.

'Yes, probably. But was it good history or bad history? That's the question.'

'Sexual tension. Couldn't you sense it?'

'Maybe. But he's married, isn't he?'

'Is he?'

'I googled him last night after the boss said he was being brought into the investigation. Happily married for fifteen years, two sons.'

'Did it actually say "happily married"?'

'Well, no, but it implied it.'

Richard shrugged. 'Wouldn't be the first or last to have an affair, happy or not.'

'Would you cheat on Pauline?'

'I'm not sure.'

That wasn't the answer Becky had expected, and her horror showed on her face. 'You wouldn't! Pauline's lovely, far too good for you.' She ended with a smile, trying to bring the conversation back to a safe place.

'Exactly. She's gorgeous, clever, has a great job. What does she see in me? She's more likely to cheat on me as the years roll by, and then who knows how I'll react?'

'Get over yourself. You can't go through life thinking like that.'

'You're a fine one to talk. What happened with you and Elliot?'

'That was nothing to do with infidelity. We'd been together since uni and just sort of drifted into marriage, but neither of us was truly happy. Even Elliot admits that now.'

They sat quietly for a moment, both thinking about what the other one had said. Finally Becky broke the silence as she opened the car door. 'Thanks for the lift. See you in the morning.'

'OK. And Becky...'

'What?'

'Ignore what I said about Pauline. I just worry that I'm not always going to be enough for her.'

'You're stupid even thinking that, mate. She adores you. God knows why, but there it is. See you tomorrow.'

Becky got her keys out and walked slowly towards the front door. Her legs were like lead, and she felt irritated with Richard. To say his attitude towards adultery had shocked her was putting it mildly. She didn't know a more together couple than Richard and Pauline; they were so obviously in love that it was sickening. Then again, if he could voice doubts like that to her it did mean that he trusted her, which in their line of work was vital. Becky put it down to the long days they were both working, and decided a hot bath and a large glass of chilled white wine would make life look a lot better.

As Becky slipped into the hallway she stopped; something wasn't right. She put her keys down quietly and walked into the front room. She looked around slowly, and then she saw it. Written on the mirror over the fireplace were the words 'YOU'RE NEXT!', with a photo of the crucified body in the park stuck underneath.

***

Wen got in at nine thirty, tired, disillusioned, and stressed.

Aran's light was on upstairs, so she didn't have to confront his look of disdain about the hours she was keeping at the moment. The last thing she needed was her brother's disapproval of her for doing her job. How on earth, she wondered, do people keep relationships going when they do this work?

Wen was aware that a lot of officers couldn't sustain long-term relationships, and that marriage to someone who understood their erratic shifts and moods was always a plus.

She had thought for a moment, just a small moment, that

she might have that with Jeff. He understood her tiredness, her feeling that a case would never be closed, her frustration. She had taken him into her heart, her world and her home. Aran got on as well with him as he did with any other human, and it had all seemed perfect.

She had known Jeff was married, but like a fool she had believed him when he said his wife had left him for another man. That they were free to be lovers. He made so much time for her — he even took her to his home, for God's sake — and there was never any sign of his wife. Wen found out later that she was working in India for three months, as a doctor for Médecins Sans Frontières, but by then it was too late.

Tonight she had to have comfort food; sod the healthy stuff. She found some Cheshire cheese in the fridge and teamed it up with crusty bread, butter and chutney, washed down with a beer.

As Wen ate her naughty meal, the day replayed itself in her head. They were no further forward, but at least Jeff had confirmed her suspicions that this was the work of one murderer, even if the evidence didn't fit the brief. At least they were only looking for one person, or maybe two people working together, for these crimes. Just that information meant Jeff's fee was worth it. They could pour all their resources into one investigation.

Wen put her head back and closed her eyes for a second, and her phone rang. Pulling it from her bag, she looked at the number, but didn't recognize it. 'Hello, DI Price here.'

'Ma'am, it's Becky Wainwright.'

'What's up, Becky?' Wen was immediately worried; her officers only ever called her outside work in extreme circumstances.

'I'm not sure, boss, but I think I might have a problem.'

17.

Wen read the message. It had been written in capitals, with a black marker pen by the look of it. The photo was one of the sets sent to the newspaper.

SOCO were buzzing around, and Wen soon realised she was in the way. Becky was in a car outside. Even though she wanted to be in on the investigation, she was a victim now. She wouldn't like being on the other side of the fence.

'Right, Norman, I want this place turned upside down. We've got to nail this bastard, and soon.'

'Yes, ma'am. I do know how to do my job, you know.'

Wen sighed. 'I know. Sorry. I'll just get out of the way, then.'

'That would be more helpful, ma'am.' Norman gave her a smile and Wen nodded to him, then went out to see how Becky was.

'You OK?' she asked as she got into the car beside her.

'Yes, thank you, boss. It was just a bit of a shock.' This was evident from Becky's appearance. She was pale, and shivering.

'I bet it was. Who else can get into the house, Becky? Who else has keys?'

'I've been thinking about that; probably more people than I'm happy with.'

'Ok, make a list and give it to me, and then we'll get you booked into a B & B.'

'There's no need for that. I've already called Elliot; he'll put me up for a night.'

Wen looked at Becky. 'Is that a good idea? Sleeping with the enemy?' She smiled as she said it.

'I'll be on the couch, ma'am. Anyway, Elliot was my friend long before he was my husband, and I hope that will continue when push comes to shove.'

'If that's what you want. Try and get a good night's rest,

and we will look at this in more depth tomorrow.'

Becky nodded. She looked drawn and tired, and Wen doubted she would get any sleep. She was just getting out of the car when Becky spoke again. 'The shampoo!'

'What?'

'The shampoo. I'd forgotten until now. When I had a shower the other day my shampoo had moved. I convinced myself that I'd done it. But I hadn't — why would I? When I looked for it, it was by the sink. Someone had been in the house then. Somebody had come into my house.'

***

Elliot looked concerned as Becky was handed over to his care by a young police officer about thirty minutes later. 'What the hell happened?' he asked, as he shut the door.

'Someone's been in the house. When I came home tonight, they had written a threatening message on the mirror.'

'What sort of threatening message?'

'"You're next."'

'What the hell is that supposed to mean?'

Becky flopped down on Elliot's settee. 'Not sure. You haven't got a drink, have you?'

'Yep. White wine?'

'That would be great.'

Elliot disappeared, and returned with two large glasses of white wine. 'What, you drinking on a school night? Naughty boy.'

It was a standing joke between them. Even though Elliot would cook for Becky and always provide alcohol when she needed it, which was far too often in his opinion, he only ever drank at the weekend, saying he needed a clear head for his work as a dispensing chemist. 'If I get one thing wrong, I could kill someone,' he would say in his defence when Becky told him he was a lightweight.

'I think this counts as exceptional circumstances,' said Elliot. 'Anyway, I'm on a study day tomorrow, so I'm not a danger to the British public.'

'How is work?'

'It's fine. But stop trying to change the subject. I want to know why my ex-wife has been brought round in a police car late at night after a break in.' Elliot looked at her enquiringly.

Becky took a long drink from her glass, and said nothing.

'Or is it not just simple breaking and entering?' Elliot continued. 'Leaving a message, what's that all about?'

'No one broke in, which is the worrying part. Someone let themselves in, with keys.'

'Which keys? How?'

'That's what we'll have to find out. And worse, it might be connected to the case we're investigating at the moment.'

Now it was Elliot's turn to go pale. 'Which one? The body in the bin, or the body in the park?'

'Both.'

Elliot stared at her. 'Both?'

'Yes. Same murderer, we think.'

He drained his glass. 'I need more wine.'

***

The next day the office was buzzing, and Wen had a job to keep order. She had tried twice to get their attention by shouting, but to no avail, so she sat and waited until at last the room became quiet. 'Thank you. Now I will tell you what has actually happened. Never mind what your mate told you, which is probably rubbish. We are dealing with facts here, so listen.'

She stood up. 'As you probably know, DC Wainwright has had someone going into her house and moving things, and last night that person wrote these words in marker pen on her mirror: "YOU'RE NEXT".' Wen wrote this on the board. 'They also left a photo of the murder scene from the park crime. So, thoughts please?'

Everyone spoke at the same time.

'One at a time PLEASE! Right, DC Jones.'

'Do we know how they got in?' Richard asked.

'Yes. They let themselves in with a key. Becky sent me an email this morning with a list of anyone who might have access to a set of her house keys.' Wen turned back to write on the whiteboard. 'She has a set, obviously, as does her ex-husband, Elliot Wainwright. So does the estate agent, and the woman who lives next door.'

'Has her ex got an axe to grind?' This came from the back of the room.

'Well, she spent last night on his settee,' said Wen, 'so I don't think there's anything there, but we will of course talk to him. What do you think about the ex, DC Jones?'

'Amicable break-up,' said Richard. 'They still get on OK, just grew apart, I gather. To be honest, boss, she doesn't talk about it much.'

'This could be his way of trying to get her back,' said another officer. 'Frighten her so she goes running back to him.'

'Could be,' said Wen. 'I'll suss that out when I speak to him.'

'The estate agent is the most likely,' said Cassie. 'Let's face it, people are in and out of places like that all the time.'

'I agree, so will you go and visit them, please. I want you to speak to everyone that works there; part-time staff, cleaners, the lot. Have they had any work done since the house went on the market? Has anyone viewed it? And Richard, you go and talk to the neighbour. Make sure she still has the keys, and find out where she keeps them. Could someone have lifted them and had copies made without her knowing?'

'Is Becky OK?' asked Richard, tapping his foot on the floor.

'Yes, she's fine,' said Wen. 'Just a bit shaken. I told her to take today off, but why don't you call her, Richard, and see for yourself. She might be glad of a chance to unload.'

***

'Why don't you stay here again tonight?' Elliot said, as he got his papers together and put them in his briefcase. 'I don't mind sleeping on the settee if you want to take the bed.'

Becky hesitated, then smiled. 'Thanks, Elliot, I might take you up on that. Forensics should have finished but I just don't like the idea of going back yet, even with new locks.'

'OK. Take my spare key, and I'll see you later.' He paused by the door and looked back at her. 'You will be OK, won't you? This whole thing has scared the crap out of me, so God knows how you feel.'

'I'll be fine. I'll pop back to the house when I've collected the new keys from work and grab some things.'

'You won't be going there on your own, will you?'

'No, I'll get Richard to go with me. Now go and do your course and stop worrying about me. I've got a whole team of highly qualified detectives to do that.' Becky smiled as he opened the door, but as soon as he had gone, she ran into the bathroom and was violently sick.

***

'Where exactly do you keep the keys to your properties?' Cassie had her pocketbook out and was preparing to take notes.

'In the safe, of course,' replied the estate agent, a pretty woman who looked about thirty-five.

'Can you show me, please?'

'Yes, if you want.' She led the way into a back office where she opened a cupboard to expose the safe.

'And can you show me Mr and Mrs Wainwright's keys, please?'

'Yes.' She hesitated for a moment. 'Can you turn round, please?'

'Really?'

'We have rules to follow as well as you, you know,' the estate agent said, with indignation in her voice.

'Yes, of course you do. Sorry.' Cassie turned away as the estate agent put the code into the safe. It clicked open, and then she turned back.

The woman was taking out several sets of keys, all labelled neatly. 'Right, let's see.' She sat down at her desk and started to go through the bundle. 'Here we are,' she said in a relieved voice, as she pushed one set towards Cassie. '28 Meadow View.'

'And that's the only set you have?'

'Yes.'

'How many keys do you hold at the moment?'

The woman raised her eyebrows at Cassie. 'Well that depends, doesn't it. If sellers want us to show prospective buyers around while they aren't in, we hold their keys.' Her voice was that of a teacher explaining a simple problem to a young child. 'These are all the keys we have just now,' she said, waving her hand at the ones taken from the safe.

'And you do that a lot, do you? Show people around?'

'More and more, usually at the seller's request.'

'But don't most people look at property in the evenings and at weekends?'

'Yes, and like Mrs Wainwright, a lot of people work unsociable hours. And many people just don't want to be in the house when people look round. Some of the remarks they make are borderline vicious.'

'Really? I didn't know selling a house was such a cutthroat business.'

'You'd better believe it. They say things like, "It's a bit small, it's a bit big, it's not decorated the way I like it, it needs too much work." You wouldn't believe they'd looked at it on the internet first.' The estate agent pushed her chair back, picked up the keys, and headed for the safe.

'Not the Wainwrights' keys.' Cassie put her hand out. 'I'll take those.'

'On whose authority?' The estate agent's lips pinched together.

'The owners, and the police.' Cassie took out an evidence bag, picked up the keys with her pen, then popped them into it. 'Who else has access to the keys, beside you?'

'No one.' The woman's face was flushed, her fingers gripped her desk.

'And no one else knows the code to the safe?'

'That's right. Oh, except for Torri.'

'Torri?' Cassie looked at the estate agent.

'She's my second in command. But she's beyond reproach.'

'I'll make that assessment, if you don't mind. Is she in today?' Cassie's tone was that of a person in charge.

'No, it's her day off.'

'If you could give me her address then, please. So, in conclusion, no one has removed the keys for any reason whatsoever, as far as you know?'

'Correct. Except for a viewing I did with one couple just after it went on the market. The keys stayed in my bag throughout, and I returned them to the safe as soon as I got back.'

'I'll need their names, please, and contact details.'

'Do I have to?' The woman was squirming.

'Yes!'

***

Richard stared at Becky. 'What are you doing here?'

'I need some stuff from home; therefore I need the new keys.'

'Right. I'll get them.' Richard went in search of the house keys and Becky sat down at her desk, surveying the murder board. It felt so wrong to see details about herself up there. 'Here we go.' Richard dangled the keys before her. 'You OK, Becky?'

'Not really.' She took the keys from him. 'I just don't understand what this guy is playing at. Two completely different murders, and then he threatens a police officer. None of it makes any sense.'

'Well, psychopaths don't always play by the rules, because they don't have rules.'

'But that's not true. Even serial killers have the same MO. This lunatic doesn't fit anything I've ever studied.'

Richard sat on her desk and spoke quietly to her. 'We won't let anything happen to you, Becks. *I* won't let anything happen to you. You know that, right?'

Richard was the only person who got away with calling her Becks. No one else dared call her that, not even Elliot. 'Yes,' she said, but without conviction.

'Anything we can do, anything I can do, just ask.' He put a gentle hand on her shoulder.

'Funny you should mention that...'

***

Elliot had had a hard time concentrating on the topics that had been discussed this morning, and was now wondering if he really needed to know the current best treatment for headlice.

He got up from his seat in the cafeteria, ready to go back to the lecture hall and try to get to grips with antacids and their side effects, when he heard his name being called. 'Mr Wainwright?'

Elliot stopped mid-stride. 'Yes?'

Wen got out her warrant card. 'DI Price. I'm Becky's boss. Could I have a quick word, sir?'

'I'm going into a lecture, can it wait?'

Wen took his arm. 'Not really. I'll buy us a coffee.' She directed him back towards the cafeteria and they sat down. 'What can I get you?'

'Nothing, thanks, I've just had a drink.'

Wen smiled and went to get herself a much-needed caffeine hit, then returned to sit with Elliot. 'Did Becky get any sleep last night?'

'I doubt it. I know I didn't. Who is this madman, and why is he scaring Becky?'

'I wish I knew. Do you know of anyone who might want to frighten her? Somebody she's pissed off?' She tore open a sugar sachet and poured it into her cup.

'No, of course not. You're more likely to know that than me.' Elliiot had never met Wen before, and he didn't know what to make of her.

'Yes, and we're looking into cases Becky has been involved with in the past, you can be sure of that. Can I ask about you two and the break-up? Whose fault was that?'

'No one's, and both of us.' Elliot looked beyond Wen, trying to remember something.

'So there was no other person involved?'

'No. We just drifted apart.' Seriously, did this woman have nothing better to do. Elliot thought she might spend her time more productively looking for the person threatening his wife.

'But am I right in thinking that Becky instigated the split?' She sipped her drink, allowing Elliot time to think about his response.

'Yes. I wasn't happy, but I couldn't see what was happening, and she could.'

'And you get on OK now?' Wen tried to make the question sound casual.

'She's staying with me; doesn't that answer your question?' On the defensive again, Elliot knew he sounded aggrieved.

'Right. Just one more thing. The house keys; could anyone have got their hands on your set since you moved out?'

'No. They're locked in the desk in my flat, and the key to the desk is on my car key fob, which I always have on me when I'm out.' Elliot patted his pocket, both as a demonstration for Wen and to make sure his keys were there, which they were. He sighed quietly with relief.

'Thank you, Elliot. I'm sorry to interrupt your day.'

He rose to go, then paused. 'How did you know I was here? Even Becky didn't know where this course was being held,' he asked, puzzled.

Wen smiled. 'I'm a police officer, sir. It's part of the job description to be a nosy bitch.'

As she walked away, and allowed Elliot to go back to the lecture hall he silently agreed.

18.

'I'll come in with you when you interview Janet,' Becky said, as they drove towards her house.

'I'm not sure you're supposed to be working this case any more, Becky. Not in the field, at any rate.' Richard had filled her in on that morning's team briefing. 'The boss wants you in the office from now on, collating info and following up leads on the phone.'

'Great!' snapped Becky. 'I'm still coming to Janet's, though. She has a right to know what's been going on. Police all over the place, and then you turning up to give her the third degree. And as for Elliot being interviewed by the DI, that's just ridiculous.'

'I think she intends it to be a friendly chat,' said Richard. 'I'm not sure she's getting the thumbscrews out just yet.' Richard indicated as they turned into Becky's road.

'Elliot won't even kill a spider; he hasn't got a bad bone in his body, Richard.' Becky sighed. 'Anyway, have there been any other leads? Has the DNA shown anything? And what about the missing men?'

'No new leads, and no results yet from the DNA. We're still waiting for the result on the blood we found in the wood. I'm going to interview the CPN at the psychiatric unit tomorrow; well, if nothing else gets in the way.'

Richard pulled up outside Becky's house. 'I'll come in with you, just to be on the safe side. Although I doubt even a lunatic will have tried to get in since you called the boss last night.'

Part of Becky wanted to say that she didn't need him to actually go inside with her, but she did. She needed that reassurance that nobody had been in, and that no one was there now.

The new key was stiff in the lock. Inside, the place didn't look as bad as Becky had thought it would, just untidy and dusty. The mirror was missing, and it didn't feel like her home any more. Suddenly she realised how it must be for victims of burglary, never feeling safe in their home; the one place where they should be able to shut their door and feel in control.

'I'll just pop upstairs and pack a bag. Won't be long.' She meant that. She didn't want to stay in this house any longer than she had to.

Twenty minutes later she was sitting in Janet's kitchen with Richard, drinking tea. Janet was a middle-aged single woman who worked as a theatre manager at a local private hospital. Becky didn't know her that well, but she was the sort of person you could chat to over the garden fence, who would take parcels in for you and feed your cat when you were away on holiday. If you had a cat, that is. Becky had given Janet a spare set of keys after she had locked herself out twice following the break-up, having grown used to Elliot nearly always being home before her.

'So someone broke in? Did they take much?' Janet asked as they drank their tea.

'Not exactly, Janet,' said Becky. 'Whoever it was let themselves in with a key.'

'Which is why we are here.' Richard put in for good measure.

'And how did they get a key? Have you lost a set, or something?' Janet looked perplexed.

'No. We don't know. You still have mine, I take it?'

'Of course.' Janet got up and went into the kitchen, returning with the keys that Becky had given her.

Richard took out his pocketbook. 'And no one could have "borrowed" them without your knowledge, Miss...'

'Woods, and the answer to your question is no. No one could have taken them without my knowledge. They are in the key cupboard next to mine, and as I get and put back my keys at least twice a day I would notice if they had gone, because they are the only other set in there.'

'Have you had anyone in doing work recently?' enquired

Richard.

'No. The last time I had workmen in was before Becky gave me her keys. I had my bathroom replaced, but that was over a year ago.'

'No gardener, no one to read the gas meter? Have you seen any strangers about, people acting suspiciously? Any cars parked that you don't recognize?' Richard fired questions at her.

'I do my own gardening, and my meters are in boxes on the outside of the house,' Janet snapped. 'And no, I've seen nothing strange.'

'I'm really sorry, Janet,' said Becky. 'It's just, well, my visitor might be linked to a more serious crime we are investigating.'

'It's fine, Becky. I understand. More tea?'

'No thank you, we need to get on. I'll take the keys if I may, Janet. They won't work now anyway, as the locks have been changed.' Becky put them carefully into an evidence bag. 'And if you think of anything else, call me. You've got my mobile number, haven't you?'

'Or on this number.' Richard presented her with his card. 'Thank you for your time, Miss Woods.'

'When will you be back home, Becky?' Janet asked as she saw them out.

'Oh, in a few days, I think.'

'Text me when you're back and I'll put the kettle on. I'm always here, except when I'm working, of course.'

'Thanks, Janet.' Becky smiled as she left her neighbour standing at the door. 'You must be joking,' she thought to herself. 'Hell will freeze over before I live there again!'

***

Wen read the report from Jeff that had just landed in her inbox. It didn't tell her anything she hadn't expected, but she would read it to the team later. Then they could pick at all the information, and look at it from a multi-disciplinary viewpoint.

But first she needed to inform Jeff of the latest development. It might alter his perception of the profile she now had.

She dialed his number and he answered on the third ring. 'Jeff Morgan.'

'Hello, Jeff, it's —'

'Why, hello Wen. How nice to hear from you. I take it you've received my report. What do you think?'

'More or less what I was expecting, but —'

'But it's better when it comes from me. People will take more notice.'

'I suppose so, but that's not what I was going to say. There's been an incident, and I thought you should know.'

***

Cassie knocked at the address she had been given for Torri Kendrick. It was a flat in a very pleasant part of town, but then Cassie expected an estate agent to live somewhere nice, just as you expected hairdressers to always have perfect hair, and doctors never to be ill.

After the second knock the door opened a few inches and a small blonde-haired woman looked at her, obviously just awoken from sleep. 'What?' Torri Kendrick was about five feet three, slim, and had a cropped haircut which emphasised her elfin face. She was dressed in pyjamas, and had makeup streaked down her face. Looking about eighteen, but probably nearer twenty-five, Torri was in a state of extreme distress.
'Sorry to disturb you, Ms Kendrick, I'm Detective Sergeant Rowden from Cheshire Serious Crime Squad.' Cassie produced her ID. 'Could I have a word, please?'

The colour drained away from the woman's face, and she opened the door a little more. 'Oh God, what's happened? Has there been an accident?'

'Please don't get anxious, no one has had an accident. I just need a quick word concerning your place of employment.'

'Oh. Thank God for that.' She stood back and opened the door to allow Cassie in. 'Sorry the place is a bit of a mess.' She looked in the hall mirror. 'That goes for me as well.'

The flat was indeed a mess. Clothes and books were scattered around, a broken glass glinted in the sunshine that trickled into the kitchen area, and two empty wine bottles stood on the coffee table, evidence of the state of the woman standing in front of Cassie. 'Have I called at a bad time?' she asked.

'You could say that. I got rid of my cheating lying bastard of a boyfriend last night. Mind you, he treated this place like a hotel. Still had his own house to run to and hide.'

'Oh.'

'Oh, indeed. Please sit. If you can find a place to, that is.'

Cassie moved some clothes from a chair and realised as she did that they were cut up into ribbons.

'That's what's left of his Armani suit. He actually cried when I did that. Not seeing me in a state of hysteria, no. All I got then was "You'll get over it. I'm doing you a favour; you deserve better than me." He's right, though. I do deserve better than him.' Torri flopped down on the settee opposite Cassie. 'I'm sorry, you don't need to hear my problems. How can I help?'

Cassie went over the same questions with Torri as she had with her boss. 'Did you let anyone have access to the keys? Could you have left the safe open when someone might have gone into the back office?'

'No. I've had nothing to do with that property, and no one has had a chance to get the keys, except...'

'Except what?'

'A surveyor was going to look at it for a couple who were interested, but the vendors turned their offer down and it never happened.'

'But someone did have the keys?'

'They did, but only for a few hours in the end. The couple were jumping the gun. Got a bit carried away, I think.'

'Who was the surveyor?'

'David Lowery,' she spat, 'the man I've just kicked out!'

19.

Wen had a lot of information to impart to her team that morning. However, most of it was tightening up loose ends, not actually furthering their investigation.

'Right folks, can I have your attention please. We've loads to get through.' She turned to the whiteboard, which was starting to look a mess; scribbles, arrows, crossings-out. She really needed to condense it into relevant material.

'First of all, the profile. I'll take you through the highlights, but you all have the full report in your files and I expect you to read it. And read it properly, not just give it a cursory glance.'

People mumbled and pages were turned.

'Normally a serial killer is defined as someone who commits three or more murders, spaced out over a period of time. Usually they use the same MO and their victims have a common denominator, though where they commit their crimes can be in a small geographical area or a wider one, which is why we have the HOLMES, the national database to check for similar crimes in different regions. However, our killer has so far not followed any of these rules apart from keeping to a small geographical area. There is nothing on the national database to suggest he has killed outside our area.' Wen paused for a moment to collect her thoughts. 'Doctor Morgan thinks the killer is a very disturbed person who has been ignored in the past and made to feel useless. He is likely to have suffered physically and mentally, he has probably been sexually abused, and he is a very damaged individual. The killer wants people to take notice, and wants to be caught, but only when the time is right.'

'Does that mean he intends to kill again?' Jake asked, from behind his bank of screens.

'Yes, at least once,' Wen said, and she was glad Becky wasn't in yet. 'But we aren't going to let that happen if we can help it. What else have we got? The DNA found in the woods was from victim number two. Forensics think the killer may have wiped his hands on the grass when he stopped to take the photos. No other DNA has helped so far, and we still haven't got names for our two victims. Jake, any news on our missing men?'

'No, ma'am. Though we did get an anonymous call to say the Pole had gone to London, so we have passed his info to the Met and immigration.'

'OK. We know he's not one of our victims; his DNA has excluded him. What about Martin Grimes? Any news on him?'

'No, ma'am,' said Richard, 'but I'm interviewing his CPN today at the mental health unit, so I might get some leads while I'm there.'

'And I have a possible suspect for copying the keys,' Cassie said from the front of the room. She had reported straight back to Wen after her interview with Torri, and now she would share with the rest of the team. 'A David Lowery, estate agent, had the keys in his possession for a few hours a couple of weeks ago. He has his own estate agency, but he is a Chartered Surveyor, and also does surveys for other agents. He can't do them for his own clients due to conflict of interest.'

'DS Rowden and I are going to have a word with Mr Lowery this morning, and see what he has to say. Jake, any more missing women that might fit our female victim?' Wen asked.

'Nothing of note, boss. A few that I'm following up, but I'm not hopeful.'

'Right, well carry on with that, and Becky will be helping you later. Right, let's get to it.'

'Where is Becky?' Jake asked Richard in a conspiratorial whisper as the team dispersed.

'She's going to do afternoons for the next week, following up leads from here. The boss thought it would be less stressful while she's staying with her ex if they weren't thrown together too much.'

'See, she does have a heart,' Jake said with a smile.

***

'Mr Lowery, could we have a quick chat, please?' Wen and Cassie held up their ID cards for the man to see.

He rose from his desk looking a little flustered. 'Yes, of course.' He led the way to his office at the back of the agency. Sitting behind his desk, he gestured for the pair to take a seat. 'What can I do for you? Though if it's about the missing girl, I've already told your other officer I can't help.'

'No. This is a different matter, sir.'

He shrugged, and appeared very uncomfortable. 'Look, I'm not ashamed of who I am but I do realise that we should have been more careful. Sex in a car isn't very dignified, and if someone saw us...'

'Sorry sir, I'm not with you?' Cassie tried not to smile at the man's discomfort.

'The car sex. Isn't that what you're here about?'

'Er, no. A completely unrelated matter, actually.' Wen frowned.

'Oh. Right.' The man swallowed hard. His face had a slight sheen of perspiration on it.

Wen looked at Cassie, and then back to David Lowery. 'Can we start again, sir?'

'Yes, I think we should.'

Wen suppressed a smile. 'You had the keys for 28 Meadow View in your possession for a short while, for the purpose of carrying out a survey.'

'Did I? Possibly. I can't remember. Let me check my diary.' He opened his laptop and tapped away at the keyboard for a few moments. 'When was this?'

'About two weeks ago,' said Cassie, consulting her pocketbook.

'Ah yes, here it is. The survey that never was. The couple selling changed their minds, or something.'

'How long did you have the keys?' asked Wen.

'Half a day, I think. Why?'

'Did anyone else have a chance to get to them?'

'No, I had them in my briefcase. I always keep keys in my

case.'

'And that is with you at all times.' Wen looked the man in the eye and held his gaze for a few seconds.

'Of course.'

'Can you tell us what did you do that day?'

'I picked up the keys from Forman and Blanchard on my way into work. I worked here for most of the morning, and when I was heading to the car to go and do the survey, I got a call to say not to bother.'

'And what did you do then?' Wen enquired.

'I came back here. No I didn't, now I think about it. I was outside 24/7 when I got the phone call, so I went in there for a coffee. Then I came back here and dropped the keys back at Forman's on my way to a viewing.'

'You had them more than two hours then?' Cassie queried.

'About three and a half, I suppose.'

'And in all that time the case never left your side?' Wen asked.

'Not at all, except when I went to the loo in 24/7. But I pushed my case right under my chair and put my coat over it.'

'Then, in theory, sir, somebody at the coffee shop could have taken them out of your case when you went to the men's room?' Wen learned forward, putting her linked hands on the desk.

'No. I have a lock on my case, and I'm the only one who knows the combination.'

'And am I right in thinking that the officer who came into the agency the other day was DC Wainwright?'

'I don't know, was it? She was pretty, and interested in a flat we're selling, but I can't remember her name.'

'Thank you for your co-operation, sir,' said Wen. 'We shall be in touch if we need to talk to you again.'

On her way to the door, Cassie looked over her shoulder. 'Torri says hi.' Unprofessional? Yes. Worth it for the look on his face? Definitely.

As they walked back to the car Cassie spoke first. 'I don't trust him. One minute he couldn't remember the request, and the next he told us about the whole morning in Technicolour.'

'Maybe he was reading from his diary, but I agree he's a slimy individual. I wouldn't trust him as far as I could throw him. But he is an estate agent, after all.'

***

'Sorry I've had to alter this appointment with you twice,' said Richard.

The man sitting across from him smiled. 'No problem, at least you let me know. I'm used to my clients not showing up, and then I have to chase them. A bit like you, really. We often have to do detective work when someone goes AWOL.'

'I suppose it is. You can even detain someone without their consent.'

'When we do that, to be fair, it's usually because they aren't able to give their consent.'

Joss Parker was about forty and seemed very laid-back. His hair was slightly too long to suit his face, and he had five earrings in one ear, and a big gauge in the other. If he ever took it out, the lobe would look as if someone had shot a big hole in it.

'So, how can I help you? I believe you wanted to talk about Martin?'

'Martin Grimes, yes. He's one of your missing clients at the moment, I believe?'

'Yes. And I'm worried about him, I won't lie.'

'That's always a plus when you're talking to a police officer, Mr Parker.'

The man laughed. 'Just a figure of speech. Call me Joss, please.'

'Any ideas where Martin might be hiding himself, Joss?'

'No. I've tried all the usual places; hospitals, dosshouses, anyone he has a personal connection with, though they're few and far between.'

'And no luck?'

'No. All I can presume is that he's sleeping rough some-where. He's done that before. But he's been off his medication for at least a week, and that worries me.'

'When he was admitted after the arson attack, did he connect with anyone then, that you know of?'

'I wouldn't know,' said Joss. 'I'm not based in the unit, though I do go and see my clients when they're in there.'

'So what do you do?'

'The clue's in my title: community psychiatric nurse. I work in the community, seeing people in their own homes and at clinics.'

'Sorry. But you do keep in touch with anyone that's ad-mitted?' Richard was trying to get his head around the workings of the mental health services.

'Yes, for continuity of care. Sometimes they trust us more than the staff at the unit, which changes all the time. I'm a friendly face that they know — well, hopefully they see me as friendly.'

'Oh, I see. I've not had many dealings with your type of work before.'

'Really? I find that hard to believe, since half the people in prison have mental health issues. Anyhow, to get back to your original question: connections. I've pulled Martin's records and while he was in last time he joined in a few classes.' Joss con-sulted the file. 'Art, drama and creative writing groups.'

'OK. Can I have the names of the other inpatients who were in those classes, and their tutors, please?'

'Yes, and no.'

Richard stared at Joss as if he had developed a second head. 'Excuse me? I need that information. This is a double mur-der investigation, *sir*.'

Joss seemed completely unmoved by Richard's change of tone. 'Sorry mate, rules is rules. I can give you the tutors' names, because I know you could get those quite easily for yourself. The inpatients, however, are a different matter, I'm afraid.'

Richard was tempted to say 'Be afraid, be very afraid,' but

common sense and not wanting to look a total idiot took over at the last second, and he remained quiet.

'If you want that sort of information you'll have to get an ADP1 . Sorry, but that's just the way it is. Civil liberties, data protection and all that.'

With that Richard got up, thanked his interviewee through thin lips, and left.

20.

Becky was finding being tied to the desk, computer and phone a drag. Strange really, because in the normal course of events she spent a great deal of time busy doing just that. The difference was that now she was completely unable to follow up any leads herself.

'DC Wainwright, you are under no circumstances to leave the ops room until further notice. Do you understand that?' Wen left no doubt by the tone of her voice.

'Yes ma'am, but —'

'No buts, ifs or ands. The only reason you've not been put on leave is that I think you're safer here than at home.'

'Yes ma'am.' Becky looked defeated.

'Becky, you have had a real and dangerous threat made against your life, and until we catch this killer, I want no chances taken.'

'Yes ma'am.'

'Right. What are you doing about living accommodation? I take it this arrangement with your ex is only temporary?'

'Yes, ma'am. I'm going to look into renting a flat. I don't want to go back to the house, and hopefully it will sell sooner or later.'

'Fine, but please take someone with you when you view these places. In fact, when you go anywhere, for the foreseeable.'

Now, as Becky sifted through information the public had phoned in and tried to pick out anything useful, she wondered how long it would be before she could get her life back. What if they didn't catch this man? Would she have to move to a different job? Would that make any difference? Would whoever it was still come after her? And why her? She felt tears prickling the back of her eyes. Not one for self-pity, even she had to admit this was getting to her.

'Excuse me, Becky, have you finished with that list?' Jake peeped over his monitors.

'What? Yes, sorry Jake.' She crossed the room and handed the documents to her colleague. 'How do you do it all the time, Jake? Don't you get bored always being in the office?'

'Nope, this is my thing. You go and catch 'em, I just point you in the right direction because of my genius.' He tapped the splint on his leg. 'Just as well, really.'

'How is it?' Becky nodded towards Jake's leg.

'Touch and go at the moment.' He didn't make eye contact, just kept looking at his screen.

'In what way?'

'If I keep it or not.' Now he turned to look at her.

Becky tried not to show the shock she felt at that statement, but realised by the expression on Jake's face that she had failed miserably. 'That bad?'

'Yep. Not healing the way it should, apparently.' Jake was quiet for a moment. 'But what can you do? At least I've got one good working leg.' Gone was the face of the carefree young man, replaced with real fear.

'Well, we're going to be office buddies for a while, so at least I can go on the coffee and cake runs for you.'

Jake smiled. Not the one most people saw, the smirk of the cocky know-it-all, but the smile a of scared young man who might soon face a terrible life-changing decision. This lasted only a moment as he met Becky's gaze again. Then it vanished as quickly as it had appeared. His game face was back in place.

The tension was broken as Becky's phone rang.'Hello, DC Wainwright here.'

'Hi, Becky, desk sergeant here. We have someone down here who wants to talk to you. She says she knows who the murdered girl is.'

***

Becky took the stairs two at a time even though she wasn't trying to get her hopes up. Probably another time-waster. She had learned in her short career that most people did want to help, but sometimes too much, and got carried away by their enthusiasm to do the right thing.

As Becky reached the bottom of the stairs, the glass doors showed a young dark-haired woman of about twenty, on the edge of her seat in the waiting area. She looked ill at ease, and her left leg jiggled with nervous energy.

'Hi, I'm DC Wainwright,' Becky said as she swept through the door, extending her hand towards the possible informant.

The woman got up, edged forward, and took Becky's hand very briefly, as if by touching her she might be tainted in some way. 'And you are?' Becky prompted.

'Andrea. Andrea Belinsky.'

'OK Andrea, if you'd like to come this way please, we can have a quiet chat.'

The woman looked uncertain, and glanced at the front door as if reconsidering her options.

'It's OK, Andrea,' said Becky. 'You're safe here. No one will hurt you, and anything you tell me will be treated with the strictest confidence.' Andrea relaxed slightly, and nodded her assent.

Becky led the way to a private room with comfy seats, a coffee table, and bright prints on the wall. They'd tried hard to make the place look non-threatening and homely, and it got halfway there, only to be defeated by the mesh on the outside of the windows. 'Please, sit down,' she said. 'Now, is it all right if I take some notes? It's so I don't forget anything that might be important.'

Andrea nodded again.

'Is your English all right? Or would you like me to get an interpreter?'

'No, thank you. My English is good, I think.'

'Well, it sounds good to me. First of all, can I take some personal details?' Once again the woman looked startled. 'Only if you want to.'

Within ten minutes Becky had Andrea's date of birth and address, that she was in the country as an asylum seeker, and was awaiting a status review by immigration.

'You're from Poland?'

'No, Russia. I defect. They will kill me if I go back.'

'Why? What did you do?'

'I can't... This was a mistake.' She stood up, beads of sweat on her brow.

Becky jumped up. 'I'm sorry. That's got nothing to do with me, or the help you can give us. Please sit down. Only questions about the dead girl now, I promise.' The woman hesitated for a moment, and then sat down again. 'Who do you think she is, Andrea?' asked Becky.

'I think she might be my sister-in-law, and if it is, the dead man, I think that's my brother.'

***

Two hours later, Andrea was taken by a uniformed officer and driven her to the squat where she had been living to pick up her few belongings, and then on to a shelter which, for the moment, would be her new home.

During that time, Becky and Wen had gently extracted as much information from Andrea as they could without scaring her into thinking they were going to interrogate her. They took her to do a formal identification of the female murder victim, and obtained a DNA sample to compare her genes with the dead man's. Andrea really wanted to see his body, and it took some persuasion to convince her it was not a good idea.

That evening, at the team briefing, they all had information to share. At last they were getting somewhere.

'The female victim is probably Katrina Belinsky, and the male we think is her husband, Luca Belinsky,' said Wen. 'Both were here as asylum seekers. They came to the UK because Luca was a scientist in Russia, and he came to this country with his wife and sister to work. They were living in a tiny bedsit until a few weeks ago, when Katrina went out shopping and didn't come back. Her husband went looking for her —'

'And he didn't come back either,' said Cassie.

'At which point Andrea, afraid that the FSB had got her brother and sister-in-law, went into hiding.'

A hand went up at the back of the room. 'Yes, Tom?'

'Sorry ma'am, but who or what is the FSB?'

'Can anyone enlighten Tom?' Wen asked the room.

'Russian secret police,' Jake called out.

Wen smiled. 'Give that man a jellybean. Yes, they're the Russian equivalent of MI5, I believe. But I don't think it was them. I reckon it was someone who knew the family and their situation, and used that knowledge to get two victims instead of one. Only one person would miss them, and she would be too scared to notify anyone in authority.'

'Perfect choice,' said Becky, grimacing. 'Even the homeless have people who'd notice if they weren't there any more.'

'Andrea only ventured out yesterday for paracetamol for a raging toothache, and she saw one of our posters,' Becky added.

'Poor woman,' said Richard. 'What's going to happen to her?'

'Hopefully she'll be able to stay in the UK, but that isn't up to us. We still can't be sure until we get the DNA results for the sister/brother match, as Andrea wasn't a hundred per cent sure the female victim was her sister-in-law. It's not easy to ID someone when you can't see their whole face,' the DI told her team

Wen's thoughts went back momentarily to the body presented to Andrea to ID, its eye sockets now covered with a piece of material to hide the horrific details from the person who had to carry out this formality. Is it true, wondered Wen, that the eyes are the soul of a person, and did her killer want to take that away from her?

'But we think it's them?' This came from Richard.

'Yes. All we have to do now is find the link. Who knew them, and knew their situation. Andrea is coming in again tomorrow, and Becky will interview her with me.'

'Shouldn't I do that, ma'am?' Cassie asked, looking rather annoyed.

'No, Cassie. Andrea trusts Becky, and I want to build on that. Now, what else have we got? Richard?'

'I need a ADP1 to get hold of some medical information, ma'am. But I've got the names of some tutors whose classes Martin Grimes took as an inpatient. I'm going to speak to them tomorrow, and hopefully by the end of the day we'll have permission to see which other patients he interacted with while he was there.'

'Good. And Cassie and I went to see David Lowery. I want to delve into his past a bit more. I don't trust the guy.'

'I was going to look at a flat with him,' Becky said, flushing slightly.

'Well, don't,' said Wen. 'Not while he's a person of interest, anyhow.' Becky nodded.

Wen surveyed her team. 'Now then, we're getting close. Go home, get some rest, and be back here at eight in the morning for a short briefing and task assignment. See you all tomorrow, and thank you.'

Becky went back to her desk. She still had a report to write up after her time with Andrea, and that would take her nicely to the end of her shift.

'How are you getting home, Becky?' asked Wen as she came out of her office.

'I've got my car, ma'am.'

'Right. I'll ask the desk sergeant to make sure someone sees you to the vehicle and waves you off.' She finished with a smile.

'There's really no need —'

'Oh yes there is, Becky. Be a good girl and do as you're told. Yes?'

Becky smiled back. 'Yes, ma'am.' It was reassuring to know that someone had her back, and in this case, it was the Warrington Police Force.

21.

After Wen got home, at a reasonable time for once, she ate dinner with her brother. He had his head buried in a book, she in a report. This was normal for the Price twins, as they both lived by the saying that polite conversation was a waste of time and energy.

Aran got up and went to the fridge. 'Would you like some more water?' He brought a bottle back to the table. It was filtered tap water decanted into a bottle with a stopper, the type that sometimes needed quite a lot of encouragement to release. These bottles lived in the fridge, so there was always cold water to drink.

Wen had argued that they could just buy bottled water from the shop, and Aran had argued that that was a waste of money which added more plastic to the already growing mountain of human detritus. Aran didn't usually lose his battles, but then he did choose them well.

'I'd rather have wine,' said Wen, and got up to help herself. Aran tutted, which she ignored. 'How's Mrs G?' Wen asked, to divert him.

'Fully recovered,' said her brother. 'But you'll have to pay her overtime to get the house back the way it was.'

'Me?'

'Yes, you. You haven't done a thing while she was off. It's your mess she has to work extra hard on.' Aran's head went back into his book. Discussion over.

Wen looked around her and couldn't see anything different. 'Yes of course, the place is a tip.' She drank some wine, promising herself more when Aran had taken himself off to his rooms. This was definitely a two-glass night.

***

'How are you?'

In another room, in another place, a second bottle of

wine had just been opened. Elliott had cooked spag bol for their evening meal, washed down with a bottle of red, and now they were sitting on the settee, their glasses replenished.

'I'm not bad,' said Becky, and meant it. 'If I think too much about what, if and why, it freaks me out. Therefore, I try not to.' She took another sip. 'This is very nice wine, but I think this glass will have to be my last. I don't want to go into the interview tomorrow all woolly-headed, and as usual I've had the lion's share.'

'Some did go into the sauce,' Elliot said, to try and make her feel less guilty.

Becky had told Elliot that they might have identified the murder victims, and that a relative had come forward with information, but that was all she had divulged. It was good to be able to tell someone who wasn't involved, though; a sort of release valve.

'So, do you think you might be closing in on whoever did these murders?' he asked.

Becky considered. 'We're closer than we were a few days ago, but as we had jack shit a few days ago that's not really saying much.' She put her glass down. 'Why, do you want your bed back?'

'What? No, of course not. I meant that this nightmare might be over for you soon. That's all.'

'Thanks, Elliot.' She leaned into him. 'I mean, for everything. The bed, the food, the support. I miss this.'

'So do I, Becky.' Was she imagining it, or did he have tears in his eyes? But then he regained his composure. 'But not enough to kill two people, which is what your boss seemed to think.'

'Sorry about that. If I said she was only doing her job, would that make it any easier?'

Elliot laughed. 'Don't worry, I know she has to cover all the bases.'

'And she did play softball with you,' Becky said, with an impish smile about her lips. 'She didn't haul you down to the nick and interview you there.'

'If that's her playing softball, I'd hate to see her playing hardball,' Elliot retorted.

'Exactly. I've a lot of people looking out for me, so try not to worry when I leave.'

He sat up and stared at her. 'Leave? Who said anything about you leaving?'

'Elliot, I need my own place. I'm going to look at a few flats to rent until the house sells.'

Her ex-husband looked dejected. 'Is there anything I can do to change your mind?'

'No. But can you come to viewings with me, please?'

'As a bodyguard, or an advisor?'

'Both.'

***

Cassie sat at home, going over the information that Becky and the DI had obtained from their new witness. She might not be privy to the actual interview tomorrow, but she wanted to be fully up to speed.

She wasn't happy that she was being sidelined for this important lead, but she had enough sense to know that the boss was right. Becky had got the woman's confidence, which went a long way when interviewing anyone, especially if that person had come from a country where interview techniques were a little different from those in the UK.

Even though Cassie had only been in the job for ten years, she'd lost count of the number of times they'd arrested someone whom the police *knew*, without a shadow of a doubt, had committed a crime, but they couldn't prove it. Apart from the death knock, the hardest part of the job for Cassie was watching someone walk out of the custody suite with a big grin on their face, the police knowing they would reoffend, and not being able to do a thing about it.

She could understand why some rogue police officers took the law into their own hands. She didn't agree with it, but she did understand their reasons. In her experience, though, doing such things only ever came back to bite you in the bum, and hard!

No, if they were going to nail this particular murdering bastard, it would have to be one hundred per cent kosher. But they needed to nail him, and soon.

***

Richard was home alone. Pauline had gone to her yoga class, and usually that was his chance to watch football on TV and down a few beers. But not tonight. He'd had an idea for a story, and decided to get it on his laptop before the muse left him.

He had written since he'd been at school. Short stories, plays — God, he'd even written some poetry once. He didn't show anyone his work, because he was afraid that people would laugh at him; big tough Richard trying to be a writer. He could just hear the guys back at the station. 'A writer? Don't be ridiculous. Takes him all his time to write a report.'

So he wrote for fun. He wrote murder stories. One day he hoped he would have the courage to try and get them published, and show everyone what he could do. That day would be so sweet.

22.

'Miss Wilson?'

'Marjory, please.' The middle-aged woman smiled at Richard as she handed him a cup of coffee. She had long blondish-grey hair which was swept up haphazardly, tendrils trying to escape at every opportunity. He observed her neat figure and small face. She looked fragile, as if she could easily break apart.

They sat in a warm, welcoming sitting room, with deep chairs and far too many scatter cushions for Richard's liking. Already one was pushing into his back, giving him the urge to toss it onto the floor as he would do at home.

'Cheers.' Richard raised his cup. He needed this drink, as he'd had no coffee for at least three hours. He took a sip, and decided he would have to leave it to cool for a bit longer. He was used to getting tepid drinks in coffee shops these days, and had burnt his mouth with the office coffee on more than one occasion because it came hot from their machine.

'Marjory, thank you for your time. Much appreciated.'

'Not at all, Detective, if you think I can help. It's all rather exciting. Oh dear, what does that say about me? Bored, single, middle-aged woman without a life, I suppose.'

Richard smiled. 'Not at all. People usually fall into two different categories where the police are concerned: terrified, or thrilled.'

'Really?'

'Well, it's a wide spectrum, but yes.'

'I see.' She curled up on an oversized chair and tucked her legs underneath her while she nursed her drink.

'I believe you teach art at the Benson Unit?'

'I did, yes. I left about six months ago.' For the first time since Richard had met Marjory Wilson, she looked uncomfortable.

'Oh, so you don't work there now. Can I ask why?'

She sat up and put her cup on a small coffee table beside her chair. 'I was assaulted by one of the patients.'

'Sorry, I didn't know. Were you badly hurt?'

'Not physically. I went into the storeroom in the art studio and a man followed me in. He tried to —' She looked away, clasping her hands tightly. 'He started touching me and pulling at my clothes.'

'Didn't anyone notice what was going on?' Richard said, concerned that a nice woman like Marjory should have to go through something like that.

'Oh yes, someone noticed. Another patient came in after him and started hitting him. I was covered in blood.'

Richard could see that reliving this event wasn't doing this woman any good at all. 'I'm so sorry. Shall I come back later in the week? The last thing I wanted to do was upset you.'

Marjory looked at him, blank-faced. Then she shook her head. 'No, I'm fine. Please, ask me what you were about to.'

'If you're sure. I wanted to ask you about teaching art. I believe you taught a man called Martin Grimes while you worked there.'

'Martin, yes. He was a very quiet man who didn't really want to be in my class. He took part, but it was very half-hearted. I think it was only because his friend went to my class, and you know I can't tell you about that, don't you?'

'Yes of course, I wouldn't ask you to tell me anything that breaks confidentiality. But these two, were they close?'

'The other man was the dominant one, Martin was very much a follower.'

They chatted for a while longer as Richard finished his coffee, the woman telling him a little more about Martin Grimes, putting meat on the bones of their missing man,

'Thanks Marjory, that's been very helpful.' Richard fished in his pocket for a card. 'If you think of anything else, please give me a ring on this number.'

She took the card, 'I will. Just one thing, though, before you go.'

'Yes?'

'The man Martin was close to… He's the man who saved me, in the store cupboard. But he almost killed my attacker in the process.'

***

Becky had the woolly head she had tried to avoid. Not from the wine she had consumed; well, not entirely. She had had about three hours' sleep altogether.

She sat next to her DI and opposite Andrea Belinsky, with her notebook on her knee. The interview was being recoded with the witness's permission, though she wasn't happy at first.

'Why?' she had asked, looking like a scared child who didn't know what was happening to her.

'It's just for our records, Andrea,' Becky explained. 'If you don't want us to record the conversation, we won't.'

Reassured by the fact she had some control over the situation, Andrea relaxed slightly and consented.

'Thank you for that. And if at any time this gets too much we can stop and have a break, just say. Is that OK?' Again, Andrea nodded. 'Now, let's go through what happened from when you first came to Warrington.'

After two hours of constructing background information on the family since they had moved to the area, there was general consensus that a break was needed.

'I'll go to the canteen and get drinks and biscuits,' volunteered Becky, glad of the chance to stretch her legs and get out of the room. 'What do you prefer to drink, Andrea? Tea, coffee or a cold drink?'

'Tea, please.' Becky took the order and left the room.

'I was the only tea drinker in the family,' Andrea told Wen. 'My brother, he drank coffee all the time. He especially liked a little coffee shop in a place called Stocken Hath.'

'Stockton Heath,' corrected Wen automatically.

'Yes, that's it.'

'That was quite a way from where you lived, though. There must have been coffee shops closer to your home?'

'Yes, but his friend worked at this one, and he would often give Luca coffee and cake for free if his boss wasn't about. He would stay there for hours, reading, or writing about our experiences, or — what is it you say? "People-watching." It made him feel we had done the right thing to leave our country and try to have a new life here.' There wasn't any sadness in her voice, just thoughtfulness. 'I wish I could remember the name.' Andrea closed her eyes, and Wen studied her. She had beautiful pale skin, and long thick hair tied back in a loose ponytail. But she was too thin. Wen wondered what other hardships life had in store for this young woman. Then suddenly her eyes opened. 'Sorry, it's gone. But it had numbers in the name. I'm sure it will come back to me.'

***

Back at base, Cassie was researching the life and times of David Lowery. She was trying not to let her instant dislike to the man cloud her judgment, but it was difficult.

On social media she found his property business, and very little else. He had been married twice but had no children, and the only photo she could find, besides pictures of him standing inside his estate agency with a sharp suit on and a sickly smile, was one taken at a recent crime-writing event at the local library. 'you think you're the next Ian Rankin, eh,' Cassie thought. She decided to visit his ex-wives and have a friendly chat, so once she had their current addresses, she collected her coat and bag. 'Let's see what your exes have to say about you, Mr Smarmy Lowery.'

***

Richard's next interview was a good hour's drive away, as the creative-writing tutor at the Benson Unit lived in Blackpool. Not a place he liked, or visited if he could help it, but today was one of those days when what he liked and disliked didn't matter.

He found William Asgard's residence in a seedy back street. Even his name sang of the melodramatic, secret life of a writer. As Richard knocked, he hoped that interviewing a real writer might encourage his hopes of being published someday. His latest story was forming into a fully fledged novel, and he hadn't run out of steam yet. Quite the contrary, in fact; he took advantage of every opportunity to sit at his laptop and get his ideas down. Even Pauline was quizzing him on the amount of 'work' he had been doing at home over the last few days. 'This case must have really got under your skin,' she commented, as she read her novel while he wrote his.

'Just research, really,' he replied, noncommittally.

'Can I help you?' A rather bedraggled man stood in the doorway. It was hard to guess his age because of his unkempt appearance, but a ballpark figure would be about mid-fifties.

'Mr Asgard? DC Jones from Cheshire Serious Crime Squad.' Richard showed the man his ID, which he peered at over glasses that had slipped down his nose.

'Ah, yes. Is that today, then?'

'Yes sir, we made an appointment when I phoned you.'

'Did we now? Well, you'd better come in then.' He disappeared into the darkness of the hallway, and Richard followed him into a bleak front room. The curtains were half-closed, but the windows were so dirty that Richard thought opening them fully would make the room only a little brighter.

The room contained a desk, a chair, and books piled up everywhere. A desk lamp shone a beam of light on a laptop, and threw everything else into different shades of grey. The author moved a stack of books, exposing a stool. 'Please sit down.' William Asgard sat behind the desk, putting his elbows on the desk and resting his chin on his hands.

'What do you think I can do for you, Detective?'

'You teach creative writing at the Benson Unit in Warrington?'

'Yes. I think we established that on the phone.'

'Just double-checking, sir, that's all. Do you teach the subject at other places as well?'

'Yes. I teach two night classes a week, and give talks at writing conferences and courses.'

'So you don't just write books for a living?'

'Detective, I don't know what you expect a published author's life to be like, but I'll have to disappoint you. Most of us can't make enough money from writing alone to pay our bills, so we do other jobs. Even then, it's touch and go whether I can make ends meet each month. This house, for example. It's my house, but I have two rooms and rent the others to pay the mortgage.'

'So why do you still do it?'

'Why indeed? I have two degrees, and one master's. I had intended to teach and write in my spare time, which I did to begin with. I even got lucky with my first novel. An agent, a publishing deal, the whole dream.'

'What happened?'

'I left the day job to concentrate on my craft; after all, I'd proved I could do it. It sold very well and got good reviews. But I didn't have a second novel in me. I've published others, of course, but they are dross. Having supped at the breast of success, I am now addicted to the hunt for the next best piece of fiction, which of course will be mine.' He laughed. 'However, I'm sure you're not here for my miserable life story.'

Richard had Googled William Asgard before his visit. His webpage presented a successful author who had written many novels, and only taught creative writing to 'give something back'. His work at the mental health unit was highlighted as a further gift, given from the goodness of his heart.

'Sorry, I was just interested.' He remembered the reason he was here. 'While working at the Benson Unit you had a Martin Grimes in your classes, is that right?'

'Among others, yes. He was quite the talent, was Martin. He wrote some beautiful poetry.'

'Really?'

'Yes. His friend, now, that was a different story. He wrote about crime, very graphic stuff. The sort of thing the public love these days.'

'Who was this, then?' Richard hoped William would let

the name slip.

'The unit called me to say you might be in touch. You know I can't tell you that.'

Richard felt his face heat up, and was glad the room was dark. 'I'll find out anyway in a couple of days.'

'From them, not me. And when you do have some names, call me back. I might have more information for you then.'

***

The last person Richard needed to talk to that day had to be contacted by phone as he was in Italy, having secured a small part in a film there.

'Thank you for your time, Mr Redmain.'

'Leo, dear boy. Not at all. Anything I can do to further the course of justice.' Richard looked skyward, glad this wasn't a video call. How do they think these names up, he wondered.

'Thank you, Leo. It's in connection with an ongoing investigation. I believe you took drama groups at the Benson Unit for a term?'

'Yes, while I was resting. A complex group, quite taxing at times.'

'How do you mean?' Richard wondered if he could tap into Leo's chattiness, and get some information that might actually help with the inquiry.

'It was a small class, six if I remember, and they ranged from complete indifference to rather too passionate. I did the assassination scene from Julius Caesar once, and the actor playing Caesar got quite badly hurt.'

'They didn't have real knives, did they?'

'Good God, no!' Leo laughed. 'They didn't have any weapons at all; they had to pretend. But he gave Caesar a heavy blow to the ribs. The man doubled over, and they had to take him off for X-rays. Broken ribs, I think. That's when I decided it would be safer working in a coffee shop, or a bookshop.'

'Can you remember the name of the aggressor?'

'Aggressor? That sounds so brutal.'

'The name, please?'

'Yes, sorry. Let me think.' Time passed and Richard tapped his foot under the table, since patience wasn't his strong point. 'No, sorry, I can't remember.'

Richard decided to try a shot in the dark. 'It wasn't a man called Martin Grimes, was it?'

'Ah, now that rings a bell. Martin Grimes, that's it.'

'He assaulted another patient?' Richard felt a rush of adrenaline. At last were they going to get a lead they so desperately needed?

'No, no, he wasn't the attacker. He was the victim.'

23

Cassie drew a blank with David Lowery's first wife, who was apparently in Italy on holiday. She was told this by the woman's neighbour after a very fierce interrogation. 'Excuse me, what do you think you're doing?' she shouted at Cassie, who was looking into the conservatory at the back of the former Mrs Lowery's house at the time.

Cassie reached into her jacket for her warrant card, only to be threatened by a garden rake. 'Not so fast, young lady. Put your hands where I can see them, or I'll call the police.' The elderly woman retrieved a mobile phone from her pocket.

'I am the police,' said Cassie.

'Of course you are. Do I look that stupid? You're casing the joint!' She glanced at the phone and started tapping at it.

'Please, madam, I am a police officer. Detective Sergeant Rowden, Cheshire Serious Crime Squad. Can I get my ID out of my pocket, please?'

'Oh, all right. Slowly, now.'

Cassie undid her jacket and opened it so that her accuser could see she wasn't toting a gun, and very slowly removed her wallet.

'Hello, which service do you require?' a much-too-cheery voice said from the woman's phone.

'Just a moment, please.' The woman snatched the ID from Cassie's hand and inspected it closely.

'Emergency, which service do you require?' This time the sentence was said with more urgency.

'Sorry. It was a mistake.' The woman ended the call and put down her weapon, then handed the wallet back to Cassie. 'I'm sorry, but you were acting very suspiciously, you know.'

'You were quite right to challenge me, Mrs...'

'Mrs White, Gladys White.'

After a conversation about Neighbourhood Watch, Cassie asked where the owners of the house were.

'Nothing awful's happened, has it? That poor woman has had a terrible time over the years. First her rotten, cheating husband, and then her illness.'

It transpired that Gladys was no fan of David Lowery, and that after he had left her next-door neighbour for a younger model, the abandoned woman had been diagnosed with breast cancer. 'She's fine now, thank the Lord, but I blame him for her illness.'

'Do you?'

'Well, they say it can be brought on by stress. He was much younger than her, you see. Only ever after her money.'

This conversation did nothing to raise Cassie's opinion of Mr Lowery, which was further confirmed when she struck lucky at the second Mrs Lowery's address.

'What's he done?' the blonde asked as she folded her arms across her chest, a sign of defence in Cassie's book on the Psychology of Human Behaviour 101.

At first Cassie didn't think she was going to get beyond the doorstep of this nice little semi in suburbia, but then she found herself sitting on a white settee with her feet on a white carpet, having left her shoes at the door on the owner's command.

'He hasn't done anything, as far as we know. We're just getting some background information on Mr Lowery and a few other people of interest, to help us eliminate them from an ongoing investigation.' Cassie gave the woman her best non-confrontational smile.

'So, what do you want to know?' The voice remained very wary.

'We just wondered what your ex-husband was like. Why you split up, maybe how you met in the first place?'

'He was wonderful at first. I worked for him. Haven't you noticed all his employees look the same? Young, blonde and naïve. Promises you the world, but when he's bored, you're history.'

Cassie looked around. The small, modern house was well-furnished and gleaming, almost a show house. 'But you got this from the divorce?'

'What makes you think that? Why shouldn't I have a house like this?'

'Sorry. Did you get anything when he left?' Even Cassie knew that you didn't walk away from a marriage without some sort of payback.

'Well, yes, I got the house, but that was only so I'd go quietly.'

'How long were you together?'

'Two years before, and one after.'

'Pardon?'

'For two years we had an affair, and it was great. But as soon as we got married, he changed. Never in, always going off on business, or to one of his stupid writing weekends. But when he hit me that was the final straw.'

'He hit you? How often?' Cassie's opinion of this man was getting worse the more she knew of him.

'Only once. I'm no one's punch bag. That's how I got the house. I promised not to go to your lot about it.'

'I see. And what about his writing career?'

'In his dreams. What he writes is sick.' The woman shuddered.

'What do you mean?'

'All about bodies being tortured and cut up. I read one once, and it almost made me vomit. Believe me, I'm well rid of him. He's got a screw loose.'

***

The team looked tired. They had been working long hours and weekends, and they needed a break.

'Good work today,' said Wen. 'We've got a lot more answers, and a lot more pieces of the jigsaw. Jake, did we get anywhere with the IP address of the person who sent the photos to the paper?'

'Yes, ma'am. The email came from a cybercafé in the

town centre. No way of tracing who sent it, and the paper haven't heard from him again since. But then he hasn't committed any more murders — yet!'

Wen gave Jake a scathing look, but he had only said what the rest of the team were thinking.

'Right. Becky, can you fill the team in on our chat with Andrea Belinsky, please.'

Becky scanned her notebook. 'The family came to England six months ago. They lived in a centre for asylum seekers in London for a while, then they were given temporary accommodation in a B&B at Winwick. Luca had been lined up to do some work for the nuclear power industry, and was just waiting for clearance and a work permit. At that point they would have moved to a house, earned a living, generally got their lives back.' Becky took a deep breath. Andrea's story had got to her. This family, thinking they had escaped from tyranny, coming to a country where they thought they would be safe, only for two of them to be brutally murdered. 'While they were waiting they were trying to fill their time. Andrea painted, Katrina spent time reading and trying to improve her English, and Luca walked around and explored the town. He even made a few friends, it would seem.'

She looked at Wen, who ended the story. 'And one of these friends took advantage of his situation, and killed him and his wife.'

***

As Wen arrived home, all the information was still racing through her mind. The Belinskys, the background on David Lowery, and the statements given by the various tutors at the Benson Unit. It all led somewhere, but it could be up a blind alley for all she knew.

She decided to have another word with Jeff tomorrow and get his opinion, but tonight she would do some more work and see if there were any links between all this information she now had.

As she opened her front door the delicious smell of frying

onions started her gastric juices flowing. Had she eaten lunch? No, probably not. What she had done was drink too much coffee.

In the kitchen Aran was making a cheese and onion pie, one of her favourite vegetarian meals. Wen wasn't a vegetarian, but Aran was, and as he did all the cooking, she just ate what he made.

'How long will it be?' she asked, as she hung up her coat and kicked off her shoes.

'About forty minutes,' Aran replied, while mashing potatoes to within an inch of their lives.

'I'll have a quick shower, then.' Wen headed for the stairs, looking forward to getting out of her work clothes and into some jogging bottoms and a loose sweatshirt.

'Oh, and by the way, Arwen,' Aran shouted from his place at the stove. 'That murderer you're looking for. I know who it is!'

24.

Wen stopped dead. Slowly she turned and looked at her brother, who was calmly transferring onions, cheese and potatoes into a casserole dish, ready for the pastry lid waiting on the worktop.

'*What?*'

'Forty minutes, so don't fall asleep in the —'

'Not that!' Wen walked back towards her brother. 'The last thing you said, just now.'

Aran looked up with a puzzled expression on his face. 'What? Oh yes, the murderer. I know who it is.' He turned back to the meal.

'Well?' Wen's voice was a squeak.

'I'll just get this in the oven, and then —'

'*Now*, Aran!' Wen shouted, inches from her twin.

Aran backed away, his eyes wide with shock. Wen hardly ever raised her voice, and never to him. But he soon regained his equilibrium. 'Arwen, I suggest you get yourself a glass of wine, since you obviously need it, and go and sit down. It will take five minutes to finish this, and then I'll explain.'

He's right, thought Wen. Five minutes wasn't going to change anything in the scheme of things. She fetched a large wine glass and filled it from the bottle in the fridge, took a gulp from it so as not to spill any, then went to sit at the table. She sat down very slowly, watching her brother's every move.

Meticulously Aran fitted the pastry lid to the pie, pinching a neat edging all the way around. That was followed by an egg wash, and finally he put the casserole dish in the oven and set the timer. Then he started to tidy up.

'Aran,' Wen said, in a pleading voice.

Aran looked at her and sighed. 'I suppose this can wait.'

He sat on a chair, and leaned on the table opposite his sister. 'You know I said a few days ago that these murders reminded me of something I'd read?'

'Yes.'

'Well, I remembered where I'd seen it. So I went on the dark web and I found what I was looking for.'

'Which was?'

'A writers' forum. Very nasty. Perverted stuff, and gruesome.'

'And what are you doing even going onto the dark web?' Wen asked.

'I wanted to see if I could. Anyway, I was just browsing for anything to do with fiction and murder, and this came up. A writer had posted a story which depicts the two murders you've been investigating almost exactly.'

Wen could feel her heart racing. 'And you know the name of this writer?'

'Well, yes and no.'

Wen wanted to shake her brother at that moment. He was as infuriating as he was brilliant. 'Aran!'

'OK, OK. His pen name is The Avenging Angel.'

'His pen name?'

'Yes. No one uses their real name on the dark web.'

'But you can find out where the post was sent from?'

'Er, no.'

'What do you mean, no? You're a genius when it comes to this stuff.'

'Arwen, it's not called the dark web for nothing. The whole point is you can't trace who says what, or where it originated from. Not even I can solve this.'

'Oh.' Disappointment flooded Wen's whole body, and she put her head in her hands and closed her eyes.

'There is something you should know, though.'

'What?' asked Wen as she looked up and took a gulp of some more wine.

'His next kill is a police officer, according to the plot, and it's going to be soon.'

***

Becky was cooking tonight as Elliot was at a late meeting. She had been safely delivered home by Richard, who had come into the flat with her and looked around before he was satisfied. 'Now lock the door behind me, and don't open it until Elliot gets back.'

'Yes, boss.'

She smiled now; it was gratifying to know she was being looked after so well. She was cooking coq au vin, with crusty bread, and they would have a glass of the nice red some of which she had put into the stock.

She had shopped on her way home, with Richard in tow, and joked that if anyone saw them, they would presume they were an old married couple. 'That wouldn't be so bad,' he had said, with a smile on his face.

Once she had put the dish in the oven, Becky fetched her laptop and searched for flats for rent in the area. She selected size, location, and price, and seven came up that met her criteria. There was even one in the same development in Stockton Heath as the flat she'd seen in David Lowery's window. That was a definite maybe. After a closer look at the specifications, layout and inclusions, she decided that in the morning she would call the estate agent and ask for a viewing as soon as possible. She'd check that Elliot could come with her, but she was sure someone from the squad would go if he was too busy.

It was nice being back with Elliot — probably too nice, if she were really honest — and she could quite easily see them drifting back together if she wasn't careful. They hadn't slept together yet, but she knew it was only a matter of time if she stayed. Then the inevitable split-up would happen all over again, and Becky just knew that it would hurt Elliot a lot more than it would hurt her.

She was lost in her thoughts when her mobile rang. 'Hello?'

'Becky, it's Joe Patel here.'

'Who?'

'Sorry, I'm a colleague of Elliot's. We met at Karen's leaving do. You don't remember me? Anyway, Elliot's been taken ill. I'm at the hospital now. Can you get here quickly, please?'

25

Wen was taking her coat off in her office as the other members of the team started to arrive back at base. It was ten o'clock at night, and she could feel adrenaline running through her like a steam train without brakes.

What was it they said about adrenaline? The hormone of flight or fright. Well, she was terrified right now. One of her officers was missing, and she had a terrible feeling about the outcome of this next chapter in the murder story.

Richard barged in. 'What the hell happened, boss?'

'Calm down, Richard.'

'Calm down! You're telling me to calm down when that psychopath has Becky?'

'We don't know where Becky is, Richard, so stop jumping to conclusions. Come on, I'll brief the team.'

Wen waited for Richard to leave, then walked out of her office behind him. Instantly, silence fell. 'It would seem that Becky Wainwright has gone missing,' she said.

Shocked faces looked at each other, and chatter buzzed again.

'Apparently she received a call from a man who said his name was Joe Patel, saying that Elliot had been taken ill at work and she needed to get to Warrington General ASAP. We only know this because Becky called Elliot's mum and relayed the message to her. When Mrs Wainwright senior got to the hospital there was no record of Elliot being admitted, and no sign of Becky.'

'Do we know whose phone the call was made from?' Cassie asked.

'Jake, start on that now, please. Who called her, and from where. Richard, did we get permission sorted to look at the Benson Unit files yet?'

'Yes, ma'am, it was sorted earlier today. I was going to get on to it first thing tomorrow.'

'Get on to it now. Wake people up if you have to. I want to know the name of Martin Grimes's best mate. Cassie, go and bring Mr Lowery in, and then search his house.'

'Yes ma'am.' Cassie went to her desk and picked up her phone.

'And we have another lead of sorts,' said Wen. 'I discovered this evening that what has happened so far runs according to the plot of a story posted on the internet. The murders, how they were done, and the threat to a police officer.'

Richard sat up straight. 'What book? Who wrote it?'

'That I don't know. The author goes by the name *Avenging Angel*. It was written last year, but only ever submitted to the dark web as far as we know.'

'Well, Jake can trace the person who posted that, surely?'

Jake put his hands up in protest. 'Hey mate, I'm good, but I'm not *that* good.'

'What! We can't trace where it came from?'

Wen held Richard's gaze. 'I have taken advice on this and it would appear, as Jake says, that it is almost impossible to find the author. We don't even know if the person who wrote it carried out

the murders. They could just be a fan. But the story said that there would be a third murder, and it think they needed that piece of information just yet. And hopefully, they wouldn't need it at all.

***

All tasks having been assigned, Wen knew that she could trust her team to get on with their work while she interviewed Becky's husband. He had phoned Wen directly to tell her that Becky had gone missing; could he be a suspect? Of course he could, and until Wen knew differently, he would be treated as such.

One of Wen's officers accompanied her to the interview room; a young DC called Colin Briggs. He was clever, enthusiastic, still wet behind the ears, but had possibilities. Wen took a seat opposite Elliot, and it was obvious from his face that he had been crying. However, Wen had sat opposite many sobbing people, so distraught that they needed medical attention, and found out later that she had been talking to the killer of the person they had wailed about so convincingly.

'Hello, Elliot, how are you doing?' she asked in a neutral tone. 'I'm going to question you under caution about Becky's disappearance. Do you understand that?'

'But why? You can't imagine for one moment that I would hurt one hair on her head, surely?'

'It's how we need to do things at this point, Elliot.' Wen nodded to Colin, who pressed a button on the recording machine. 'Elliot Wainwright, you do not have to say anything, but it may harm your defence if you do not mention, when questioned, something which you later rely on in court. Anything you do say may be given in evidence. Do you understand?'

After adding the time and date they began.

Elliot nodded

'For the recording, can you answer, please?'

'Yes, I understand.' This was said between gritted teeth.

'Right. Tell me how you realised that Becky was missing.'

'I've already been through all this with you on the phone.' He almost shouted the words.

'Yes, but we need to look at the information in more depth. Elliot, I know this is hard, but all we want to do is find Becky alive.'

Elliot began crying again, but he managed to calm himself and answered Wen's question. 'My mother called me to ask if I was OK.'

'And how did she call you?'

'On my mobile, of course.' His impatience was palpable.

'Where was your mobile?' Wen asked, her voice direct, without emotion.

'In the pocket of the lab coat that I wear at work. She had called a few times by the time I picked up, because I'd been in a meeting for an hour, and my coat was hung up in my office.'

'You didn't take the phone into the meeting?'

'No, we're asked not to. And we can be reached by land-line for anything important.'

'And I'm presuming your mother didn't know that number.'

'Well, no.' He met Wen's gaze, his eyes haunted.

'Did Becky?'

'Yes, but she never used it.'

'What did your mother say?' impatience was creeping into Wen's questions by now.

'That she'd had a call from Becky to say I had been taken to hospital and it sounded urgent.'

'But Becky didn't try your mobile?'

'No.'

'What happened then?'

'I tried to call Becky, but it just went to voicemail. I kept trying from my car as I drove home, but still nothing. When I got home there was food in the oven, and the kitchen was its usual mess after Becky had been cooking.' At this he smiled briefly. 'But Becky wasn't there.'

'And what did you next?'

'I went outside to see if her car was there. She had to park it around the corner while she was staying. And it was, but her car keys were on the pavement. That was when I panicked and called you.'

'Your mother said Becky mentioned one of your colleagues had phoned her, Joe Patel. Is that right?'

'Yes, that's what Mum said, or at least that's what she thought Becky said. She was in a bit of a flap by this time, as you can imagine.'

'Do you have a colleague called Joe Patel, or know someone of that name?'

'No, I've never heard of him.' Elliot sat back and pushed his hands through his hair.

'What did you do then?'

'I phoned you, and you said to come to the station. I've

been trying Becky's phone every five minutes, but nothing. What do you think has happened to her?'

'We don't know, Elliot.'

'Well, sitting here asking me stupid questions isn't going to find her, is it?' Elliot's voice had risen in volume, and he was staring at her. 'He's got her, hasn't he? He's going to kill her, isn't he?' The desperation in Elliot's voice was pitiful.

Wen touched the hand of the wreck of a man in front of her, and for the first time during the interview her stern facade cracked. 'We don't know anything for sure, Elliot. I just know we need to find Becky, and quickly.'

As she walked back to the squad room with Colin, he asked why Becky hadn't called Elliot to check if he was OK. 'It's strange that she didn't try to contact him.'

'I've been thinking about that too,' said Wen. 'Maybe she just didn't get the chance.'

***

Richard had been on the phone to the Benson Unit for twenty minutes now, and felt like he was getting the runaround. He had been put on hold four times, redirected five times, and was now waiting to hear from the night manager, who was apparently dealing with an incident.

'This is urgent,' he insisted, as he was told yet again that his message would be passed on to the person in charge, and that they would get back to him as soon as possible.

'So is the incident, Detective,' was all he got in the way of a reply, and then they hung up on him.

'Oh, fuck this.' He slammed the phone down and got up. Grabbing his coat, phone and keys, he headed for the door. 'I'm off to the Benson Unit,' he called to anyone who might be listening.

***

Cassie knocked on David Lowery's front door. It was now 11 pm, and she had two other cars full of officers with her, plus the three in her car. Blue lights illuminated Lowery's drive like a Smurfs' disco.

After a second round of hammering on the door with no effect, Cassie was just about to give permission to break the door down when a very bleary-eyed man opened it about six inches. 'What the hell is all this?' he managed to slur.

'Mr David Lowery, I'm arresting you in connection with the disappearance of Rebecca Wainwright.'

As Cassie continued with the caution the man's face took on a look of complete disbelief. 'I don't know what the hell you're talking about,' he muttered.

'Can you go with these officers, sir, while we search your house. Thank you.' Cassie flashed the warrant at David as he was led away. 'Right guys, let's turn this place upside down.'

**

'Nothing?' Wen felt she was grasping at straws.

'No, ma'am,' said Cassie. 'We found nothing to make me suspect that anything abnormal had happened in that house. SOCO are there now, dusting for fingerprints and looking to see if we missed anything. However, we did find these.' Cassie held up an evidence bag with a collection of keys inside. 'We've checked, and one of them is Becky's front door key.'

Was this finally the light at the end of the tunnel? 'Right then, let's go and have a chat to Mr Lowery. Our doctor has said he's OK to interview, now that we've poured several cups of black coffee down his neck. I think throwing up might have helped, too,' said Wen, with a slight smile.

Down in the interview room, where only a few hours before she had sat opposite Elliot Wainwright, she now faced a sorry-looking David Lowery. He was pale, red-eyed, and his breath would have taken paint off a surface at fifty yards.

'How are you feeling now, Mr Lowery?' asked Wen, though as long as he could be questioned, she didn't give a damn about his wellbeing.

'I feel like shit. And I want a lawyer. I'm not well enough to be here.'

Wen had anticipated this, and had already contacted the duty lawyer to come in. 'Of course.' She nodded to Cassie, who left the room and reappeared moments later with a guy who looked marginally better than Lowery. He unbuttoned his crumpled jacket and sat down.

'Hello, Mr Lowery. I'm Robert Shepheard, duty solicitor.'

'I don't want him. I want *my* solicitor, Penelope Milton.'

There was nothing they could do. Lowery had the right to legal representation of his choice. But if his, no doubt, expensive lawyer didn't get her arse into the station quickly, Lowery would have to go with what was on offer.

Frustrated by the delay, Wen and Cassie went back to the office and got coffee. 'Let's go over what we have,' Wen said to Cassie as they sat down in Wen's room. Jake had told them as they came back into the office that he had traced the call made to Becky. It had been from a pay-as-you-go mobile, outside Elliot's flat, and it hadn't been used since. Neither had Becky's mobile.

'I wonder what Richard got from the mad hospital,' said Cassie.

Wen gave her a scathing look. 'I take it you and your loved ones have never suffered from mental health issues.'

Cassie looked slightly embarrassed and got up. 'I'll go and ask him.' She went into the main room and looked around for her colleague. 'Anyone seen Richard?' she asked.

There were a few shakes of the head before the DC who sat next to Richard came off the phone. 'He's gone out somewhere,' she said.

'Where?'

She shrugged her shoulders. 'Sorry, Sarge, I was on the phone.'

Cassie walked over and looked in the office diary. Staff had to sign in and out and write down their whereabouts for safety reasons, but there wasn't anything written by Richard's name.

Just then another officer came into the room. 'Eric, you don't know where Richard went, do you?'

'Yes, Sarge, smoke break. He mentioned Benson and

Hedges.' Eric frowned. 'I didn't know he smoked.'

'He doesn't, you prat. He probably said the Benson Unit.'

'Oh yeah, that was it.' Eric thought. 'But that was ages ago. He should be back by now.'

Cassie didn't like that at all. She looked up the number of the unit, and it rang ten times before anyone answered. 'Benson Unit, Charge Nurse Jackson. How can I help you?'

Cassie introduced herself. 'I believe one of our officers was coming to see you for access to some case notes.'

'He rang, definitely, but I didn't know he was coming over. I was going to call him back, but we've had a few problems tonight and I've only just sat down.'

'You mean he hasn't been to see you?'

'No one from the police has been here in the last few hours. He did email the ADP1 over, and I've just got the relevant files out.'

'Detective Constable Richard Jones definitely hasn't been to see you in the last few hours?'

'No, he hasn't. It's a bit like a police station here, officer; you can't just walk in and out. We're in lockdown at the moment, anyway; we've had an incident here this evening.'

'Yes, so I believe. Nothing serious, I hope.'

'Serious enough. I was going to call you, anyway, as one of your suspects has been here tonight.'

'What do you mean?'

'Martin Grimes.'

'Martin Grimes? He's with you?'

'He was, until he attacked a member of staff with a knife and then tried to hang himself.'

26

'Martin Grimes is in hospital, and Richard is also now missing?'

'Yes, ma'am.' Cassie was close to the edge. She swallowed hard and cleared her throat.

Wen ran her fingers through her hair. 'What the hell is going on, Cassie? To mislay one police officer is bad luck, but two? That's just ridiculous.' She pushed herself up from her seat. 'Where does Richard usually park his car?'

'Wherever there's a space, ma'am. Sometimes on the street. You know what parking's like round here.'

'Let's take a look at the car park CCTV. If he was parked on the road, we'll have to see if anything's been captured on the street cameras.'

Together they looked at the footage. Sure enough, they could pinpoint Richard getting into a pool car in the staff car park and driving off at 10.20 pm. 'Get his plate circulated,' said Wen. 'I want all uniformed officers to start looking on the route from here to the Benson Unit. Did we get the information from the unit?'

'Yes, we did,' Cassie replied. 'The manager gave me names, dates of birth and contact details, and he's sending through case notes as we speak.'

'I want everyone on that list visited straightaway. Can I leave that to you?' Cassie nodded. 'Good. I want to get back to our guest downstairs.'

With a little help from Jake Cassie logged on to Richard's computer, to look for anything connected with Martin Grimes and the Benson Unit.

Over the phone, the unit manager had given her the names of six former inpatients who had attended the same courses as Martin Grimes. None of them meant anything to Cassie, so now she was searching for any sort of lead to help her prioritise the house calls. Those would take up a lot of time and resources, and right now they were acutely short of both.

Nothing jumped out at Cassie from Richard's input. She was just about to close the file down when she saw a note about the creative writing teacher. *Call Asgard once I have inpatient names — says he might have more info then.* Cassie stabbed in the attached telephone number and tapped her pen, waiting for her call to be answered. Eventually it went to voicemail. She tried again. Still no answer. 'Right, one more go and then I'm getting the locals to go round and kick his door in,' she said to herself.

'Hello? What is so fucking important that I have to be woken at this hour?'

Cassie was relieved to get some sort of response, even a bad-tempered one. 'Is that Mr Asgard?'

'Yes!'

'I'm sorry to disturb you, sir, but this is a matter of some urgency. My name is Detective Sergeant Rowden, and I work for the Cheshire Serious Crime Squad.'

'Oh yes. One of your men came to see me about Martin Grimes.'

'Yes sir, DC Jones. You told him to contact you again when he had names, and you might be able to help further.'

'I did.' A pause. 'And do you have them now?' Cassie could almost hear him lick his lips in anticipation of his role in this investigation.

'Yes, sir. If I read out the names, can you tell me if anyone rings any alarm bells.' Cassie referred to her notes. 'Alan Grove?'

'No.'

'Peter Rosenbloom?'

'No.'

'Damian Anderson?'

'That's the one. I remember the others, of course, but he's the one Martin adored. If Damian had told Martin to jump off the roof he would have done it without a moment's hesitation.'

'Right. Thanks for that Mr Asgard, it's really helpful.'

'Oh, but that's not what I was going to tell your colleague.' Again there was a gleeful sound in his voice. He was enjoying this.

'No?'

'The staff of the unit could have told you that, and probably will. No, I have something more.'

Cassie sighed. If this man was going for the dramatic effect, it was wearing thin. 'And this was?'

'Damian Anderson had a real gift as a writer, so I gave him the name of my agent. I thought that sort of talent should be encouraged.'

'And...?'

'Big mistake.'

'How so?'

'Dora called me about four weeks ago and gave me a real dressing-down. She was furious.'

'Why?'

'Why, because I'd given her name to a psychopath. Her words, not mine. Apparently he'd sent her some work which she wouldn't touch with a bargepole. Too dark and brutal for her. But he didn't take rejection too well. He started threatening her, and I think it really frightened her.'

'And what happened?'

'It just stopped. She told him she would report him to the police, and that worked.'

'Can you give me her contact details please, Mr Asgard? I think I need to talk to your agent myself.'

***

'Mr Lowery, how are you now?' Wen asked, playing for time as she sized up her opponent. Not the very nervous man she wanted to question, but the legal representation now sitting beside him. Wen had heard of Penelope Milton, but never had any dealings with her. That was about to change.

Ms Milton looked as if she was in her late thirties, small but perfectly formed, with a pear-shaped face and short red hair that made her look a little like a ginger cat. Considering she had only been called twenty or so minutes ago, she looked immaculate and had a full face of makeup. Nothing garish; this was so subtle it was almost natural, apart from the bright red lipstick on her very full lips. Wen wondered where the Botox ended and the plastic surgery began.

David Lowery gave Wen a contemptuous look. 'Can we just get on with this. I want to go home and get to bed.' He folded his arms and turned slightly towards Penelope. Away from his prosecutors, and towards his saviour.

'Can you tell me where you were between eight o'clock and the time my officers arrived at your house, please?'

'I was at home, getting pissed.'

'When was the last time you saw Detective Constable Rebecca Wainwright?'

'What? Who the hell is that?' Lowery hung his head as if it was too heavy for his neck to support.

'You know who I'm talking about. Our detective. She came to see you a few days ago about one of our cases.'

Penelope Milton interjected. 'I don't like your tone, Detective. My client is not well enough to be interrogated like this.'

'It's Detective Inspector to you, Ms Milton, and this is an interview. I think you'll find the secret services are the ones who carry out interrogations.'

'It's OK, Penny, I'll answer the question. Yes, someone did come, but I see lots of people. How do you expect me to remember them all?'

'I think you'd remember her. Petite, blonde, just your type. What happened, David? Did you turn on the charm? Didn't it work this time? Did she reject you?'

'Enough! This line of questioning is not acceptable.' Penelope Milton hit the desk with her hand.

Wen completely ignored her. 'Where is she, David?'

'I don't know who you mean.'

Wen pushed a photo of Becky towards Lowery. 'Oh, her!'

he said.

'Yes, her. Remember her now, do you?'

'Yes, now that you've shown me her photo. Lovely girl.'

'*Lovely?*' Wen banged her fists on the table and both David Lowery and his brief jumped. 'I'll ask you again, David, where is she?'

He moved his chair back, trying to distance himself. 'I don't know!'

'I must protest, Detective Inspector, the way you're talking to my client is unacceptable. Have you got any evidence? Either you charge him, or we are leaving.'

'Ms Milton, your client has a history of soliciting young women for sex. He has been physically aggressive in the past, and he had the key to my detective's house in his possession.'

'Had the keys, had!' cried David Lowery. 'We've been through all this.'

Wen pushed the evidence bag forward, 'For the recording, I'm showing Mr Lowery evidence item number 243-A. Do you recognise these, sir?

'No. never seen them before.' Once again Lowery looked down at his feet.

'That's strange, because my officers found these in your house when we searched it.'

'Well, they're probably just old keys I've kept from previous places I've lived.'

'Maybe,' said Wen. 'But one of them is a key that fits the front door of Becky Wainwright's house; a key you already admit to having had in your possession at one time.'

He looked at his solicitor for advice and she whispered into his ear, then straightened up. 'My client has no comment to make about this, and I would like to consult with him before this interview goes any further.' Penny Milton smiled at Wen.

Wen carried on regardless. 'Oh, and then there's the dodgy writing.' She glared at Lowery. 'Isn't there?'

'What about my writing? I've got nothing to hide. I'm part of a crime writers' group, if that's what you mean.'

'Do you share all your work with the group? What about the stuff you shared with your second wife? The stuff that you put on the dark web?'

Penelope Milton put her hand on David Lowery's arm. 'Say nothing, David.'

But he was on his feet. 'What? What the hell are you on about?'

'The second Mrs Lowery was sickened by what she read. She said it was the work of a madman.'

David Lowery laughed. 'Oh, she's a wimp. Couldn't even watch a horror film without feeling sick. Come on, Inspector, you know as well as I do that crime fiction can be disturbing. What I write is nothing compared with what actually happens. Look at these two murders you've got on your books. I mean, that girl had her eyes gouged out, for God's sake.'

'And how do you know about that?'

He looked uncomfortable. 'I read it in the papers.'

'That's strange, Mr Lowery, because we didn't give out that information. So how do you know?'

'I don't know. Someone must have told me.' Lowery squirmed.

At last she was getting somewhere. Lowery squirmed, and his solicitor looked at him. Now to press home.

Wen took a breath to go in for the kill, and her phone pinged. She glanced at it. A text, from Cassie. 'He's not our man.'

27

'This had better be bloody good, Cassie,' Wen growled. 'I had him on the ropes then.'

'Sorry boss, but he's not the murderer. It's a guy called Damian Anderson. He was in all the same classes as Martin Grimes, and Martin had a thing for him. He was a weird one, to say the least.'

'Someone being weird isn't a criminal offence, Cassie. If it were, half the country would be locked up.'

'No, it's his writing. This creative writing teacher told him he had real talent and directed him to his agent. She wanted nothing to do with his stuff, and then he started harassing her. Wouldn't take no for an answer. I've just spoken to her and she said his work was much too dark for her. I asked in what way, and she described a murder scene he had written. A woman tied to a climbing frame as if she had been crucified, disembowelled, and —'

'Her eyes gouged out?'

'Yes. He's our Avenging Angel. I'm sure of it.'

'Not just a fan.' Wen said this more to herself than Cassie. 'No. it feels... It feels personal, as if he needed to prove something.' She paused. 'So why didn't this woman make the connection when she read about the case in the newspapers?'

'She's been in Mexico for the last three weeks. She only got back two days ago, so she had no idea about these murders.' Cassie was tapping her right foot as she spoke.

'But there's no clue to what happens next?'

'No. He sent the first three chapters, and she didn't want to see any more than that. The Benson Unit sent his file through. Paranoid schizophrenia, with delusional episodes, and prone to violent outbursts. In fact he attacked a fellow-patient while he was in the unit with Martin. Someone got frisky with one of the female teachers. Damian took exception to that, and let his fists do the talking.'

'Now, you see, that doesn't make sense. Why would a sadistic psychopath help a vulnerable woman?' It was at times such as these, even though they were, thank God, few and far between, that Jeff's input would be invaluable.

'No idea.' Cassie shrugged. 'Maybe that's were being mad comes in.'

Wen considered. 'Get a small team, go to the last known address, and bring this guy in. I'll take young Colin with me to visit Martin Grimes in hospital. I just hope he can give us some useful information, because we're running out of time.'

***

It was dark, and cold. Becky didn't know where she was, or how she had got there. As she tried to move, she realised she was tied hand and foot and had tape over her mouth. She tried to sit up, but there wasn't room. She couldn't even straighten her legs. She felt sick, but knew she mustn't vomit; if she did, she might choke. She swallowed hard and tried to breathe deeply through her nose.

Whatever drug she had been given started to take effect again, and she felt the thankful relief of drifting off to sleep. Maybe this was just a nightmare, and next time she woke up it would be over.

Or maybe she wouldn't wake up at all, and it would still be over.

***

Wen hurried towards the mental health unit at Warrington General, Colin Briggs trying to keep up. As they reached the locked door of the unit Wen pressed the bell far too hard and for far too long, as was shown by the cross face of the nurse on the other side of the glass. She pointed to her watch and mouthed 'You can't come in.'

Wen took out her warrant card and held it up to the glass. 'Yes I can,' the DI said, leaving no doubt of her intention.

The nurse looked confused, then punched in a code and opened the door just enough to stick her head out. 'What do you want at this time of night that can't wait till tomorrow?' she snapped.

Wen looked at her own watch. 'It is tomorrow, so let us in, please. This won't keep.'

The staff member reluctantly stood to one side and let them pass. 'Who's in charge here?' Wen asked.

'Charge Nurse McKendrick. Shall I get him?'

'What a good idea.' Wen wasn't usually this sarcastic — she normally left that to Cassie — but her patience was wearing thin, and her fear didn't help.

The nurse disappeared and didn't return. Instead a large guy in blue scrubs appeared, his hands in his pockets as he ambled towards them. When he got within spitting distance he stopped, smiled and held out his hand. 'Phil McKendrick. Can I just check your ID again, please, and while I do that can you both sign in please?'

He took the warrant cards and carefully inspected them, then once the officers had signed the book, he gave them back with a crooked smile on his face. 'So, what can I do for you? Must be important to bring a detective inspector out this late.'

'It is sir. I believe you have recently admitted a Mr Martin Grimes from the Benson Unit?'

'Yes, we've not long got him settled. Why?'

'We need to talk to him, please.'

'Sorry, that isn't going to happen. Martin is heavily sedated, and he won't be talking to anyone for a while.'

'Oh, shit.' This was a quiet curse. Wen closed her eyes hoping that might help her focus. 'Can I at least see him?' It wasn't that she didn't believe the man, but she wanted to see how true his statement was for herself.

The charge nurse shrugged. 'OK. Follow me.' He led them down the corridor and in a room next to the nurses' office was Martin Grimes. He had soft restraints on his wrists, and an oxygen mask covered his bruised face.

'When will we be able to speak to him?'

'in about eight hours is my best guess,' the nurse said as he leaned against the wall.

Wen didn't take her eyes from the man in the bed, hoping that by staring at him she would somehow get him to open his eyes and answer all the questions whizzing around in her head. 'What happened?'

'The best person to tell you that is downstairs in A&E, getting stitched back together.'

Wen looked at McKendrick, her face puzzled.

'The nurse he attacked with a scalpel.'

***

Cassie arrived at her destination. No lights, no movement, no sound. She hammered at the door and waited, probably not for as long as she should, before giving one of the officers the nod to batter down the door with the big red key. Once the lights were on, the small team went in separate directions. Nothing, just a dull little terraced house, nothing out of the ordinary; neat, tidy, basic.

'Boss, up here,' one of the men shouted from upstairs.

Cassie took the stairs two at a time and found the officer standing in the doorway. As Cassie went into the room she stopped in her tracks. Photos of the dead woman were everywhere. Some pictures had been taken while she was alive, and showed her looking at something which obviously terrified her. But what?

'Ma'am.' Another officer appeared at the bedroom door. 'Ma'am...'

'Yes?' Cassie answered, still gazing at the photos, 'What is it?'

'You're needed in the kitchen.'

Cassie went back down, still trying to take in what she had seen upstairs. 'What is it?'

The officer didn't say anything, but nodded towards the fridge. Cassie opened it, and peered in. 'Right, get SOCO here now. And let's wake up Mr Anderson's neighbours, shall we.'

Cassie backed out of the small kitchen and into the hallway, where she got out her phone and called her DI. 'Ma'am, he's our man. He's not here, but Katrina Belinsky's eyes are.'

***

Wen received the news with mixed feelings. They knew who their killer was, but *where* he was more important now.

In A&E Wen and Colin were directed to a cubicle where the nurse assaulted by Martin Grimes was being treated. They peeped behind the curtain, where a pretty woman in uniform was putting the final suture into the last wound. 'I'll come back and clean up later.' she said, as she applied a sterile dressing to the man's forearm. She peeled off her gloves, put them into a yellow bag hanging on the side of the trolley, and pushed it out of the way.

'Thanks,' said Colin as she squeezed past him.

'How are you, Mr...' said Wen as she held out her hand.

'Bunter, Mike Bunter. I'd shake hands, only everything hurts at the moment.' He smiled as he sat up on the bed, then winced. He was a mess, with dressings on his face, arms, and hands. When they had spoken to a doctor, he had said Mr Bunter had multiple minor lacerations, with five needing suturing.

'Can you tell us what happened, please?' said Colin.

'Martin turned up at the unit about ten and stood outside, crying. We went to fetch him, and he came into the unit as if he was in some sort of trance. I took him into one of the side wards to try and get some sense out of him. That was when he flipped and pulled the knife.'

'The scalpel?'

'Yes. He started slashing at me, shouting that he hadn't killed them but he couldn't stop them screaming at him. Then he took some cord from his pocket and climbed on a chair and the next thing I knew, he was dangling.'

'And while this was going on, what were your colleagues doing?'

'They came straight away but I'd collapsed against the door, so they had trouble getting in. It all happened so fast.' Mike Bunter shivered; he had turned pale.

'I think you'd better lie down again,' Wen said. 'Colin, go and get someone.'

Colin slipped out of the cubicle, and Wen thanked Mike Bunter for his help.

He opened his eyes and looked at Wen. 'He shouted something just before he kicked the chair away.'

'What did he say?'

'This is for the Avenging Angel.'

28

No air. There was no air. She couldn't breathe properly.

Becky was on the edge of total panic. How long had she been here, wherever here was?

The last thing she could remember was talking to Elliot's mother. She was standing next to her car, just about to try Elliot's number, and feeling silly because that was the first thing she should have done. A stabbing pain in her arm, then nothing.

How could she have been so stupid? She was a highly trained detective, not just some plank off the street. Tears welled up in her eyes. Was this it? Was this where she was going to die?

No! She had to snap out of this. People would be looking for her; they'd know she was missing. Hope, that was what she needed right now. Becky knew that when one of their own was in danger the police found a way. It wasn't always strictly legal, but when a fellow officer was at risk rules were bent and lines were crossed. If they didn't find her, it wouldn't be because they hadn't tried everything they could.

Just as Becky felt a sliver of positivity creeping into her addled brain, she was jarred back to reality. A crack like thunder drove her back to the edge of terror as the lid of the container was ripped open and light flooded her world.

***

'Any leads?' Wen asked Cassie as they walked towards Damian Anderson's house.

'No, ma'am. We've done a door to door, and all we're getting is "quiet type, kept to himself, pleasant enough, polite". You get the picture.' Wen nodded.

As they reached the front door they were handed white paper suits, gloves and overshoes. Wen sighed; as if she had time to mess about with all this. But she knew that if they ever got this bastard into court, they had to follow protocol and do things by the book.

She nodded to Norman as they stepped carefully out of the way of the SOCO team, who seemed to fill this small house beyond its natural capacity. 'Have you found any clues to where Becky might be?'

He shook his head. 'Not so far, ma'am. But this guy is off his trolley. Lots of notes, and drawings of scenes for a film, or a book?'

'A book,' said Wen. 'Where are they? I want to see them.'

'In here.' Norman led the way into the front room, where Cassie had searched. On the coffee table sat a folder.

'Where was that?' said Cassie, frowning. 'I looked in here, and I didn't find anything.'

Norman pointed to the corner of the room, where some floorboards had been lifted. 'Don't worry, Sarge. We don't expect you to take the place apart, that's our job.'

Cassie felt relief flood over her. If anything had happened to her colleagues because she'd missed something obvious, she would never have forgiven herself.

Wen picked up the file, sat on the edge of a tatty armchair, and flicked through the pages. There were pencil drawings of places, and sketches of bodies hung up like slaughtered animals. Then she turned over the next page. 'Oh, fuck!'

Wen was looking at a very good likeness of her detective constable, tied to a post, covered in wounds, and the face fixed in what looked like a scream. But it wasn't Becky. The drawing showed Richard.

***

Becky had been dragged out of the box by her hair. Now she sat tied to a chair, the tape ripped from her mouth, facing an even more terrifying scenario than before. 'Dear God!' she croaked. 'Why are you doing this?'

She looked at her kidnapper, but with the bright lights behind his head she could only make out his silhouette. In front of her, tied by his hands to a metal ring high on a stone column, was Richard. He was unconscious, probably drugged as she had been, though she couldn't think how this man had overpowered her partner. Richard was as big and muscular as she was small and birdlike.

'How are you feeling, Detective Constable Wainwright?' the man asked.

Becky struggled, but couldn't move an inch.

'Not too good, I suspect. Got a headache, feel a bit sick. It does that to you, ketamine. One quick jab, and it works. Now Richard here needed a hefty wallop on the back of the head. I think I might have hit him a bit too hard, because he's been like this for hours.' He laughed.

'It was hard work getting him up there without my little helper; it took a lot out of me. Worth it, though. I know, let's see if he responds to pain.' Without another word the man went up to Richard's inert body and Becky saw the flash of a thin metal blade. Their captor put the blade against Richard's chest and pressed lightly. Becky screamed as bright red blood oozed from the wound, and Richard cried out in pain.

'That's a good sign. They test brain-dead patients with pain to see if they have any reaction, you know. They drop icy water into their ears. But this is much more fun, don't you think? Much more ... colourful.'

He made another incision, this time on Richard's underarm, and it was then that Becky realised Richard was naked.

***

The team sat at their desks, each with several pages from the file. All wore gloves, and searched each piece of artwork, each page of writing, to see if it gave any clue to where their colleagues might be.

Jake had managed to get into Damian's computer, but it hadn't been easy. 'Someone who posts on the dark web will protect their files. I can't get into some parts, that'll take longer, but what I have managed to see are his emails. Lots of dialogue with literary agents. They turn down his work, he gets angry, and so on. This guy doesn't take rejection well. Writes under a different name when he deals with literary agents. Dante Black.'

'Ma'am,' called Colin across the room, 'there's a reference here to a cellar where he takes his victims.'

Cassie and the DI were at his shoulder before he had finished speaking. Wen took the sheet from Colin and inspected it. 'Now we need to find out where this cellar is.'

'Just a mo.' Cassie took out her pocketbook, 'That's it. One of his neighbours said he worked at a coffee shop, but she didn't know which.'

Wen rubbed her eyes, 'that isn't much help. Anyway, do coffee shops have cellars?'

'Well, some will,' Cassie shot back, 'just like some houses have cellars.'

'Right, listen up everyone. We're now looking for the name of a coffee shop. Look through it all again, and see if you can link any of the dialogue with a possible name. Tell me about any place that might be worth investigating further.'

***

Richard was drifting in and out of consciousness now. Each time he was cut he seemed to come further out of his state of oblivion, and with what was happening to him that wasn't necessarily good.

'Why are you doing this to us?' sobbed Becky. She didn't know how much more she could take, and it felt like this was just the beginning.

'Because I can.' Richard's persecutor sat down in the shadows. 'Because they didn't believe it could be done. They said it was too far-fetched. Not realistic enough, not believable, more horror than crime, they said. What do they know? And now I've shown them it was possible, after all. My little friend Martin and I showed them, but it was mostly me.'

'They didn't understand you, do they?' Becky tried to reach out to this deluded wretch.

'No. And now they'll be sorry they didn't sign me.'

'Well, you are obviously talented.'

He stood up and came over to Becky, his face just a few inches from hers. She could feel his breath on her face. 'Very clever, Becky, very clever. Get on his side, make him connect with you. You're very good. But I'm sorry, that won't work.'

As he went back to Richard, Becky struggled with a thought. She knew that face. But from where?

'I think we might up the ante now. What do you think, Becky?' He took hold of Richard's testicles and twisted hard. Richard screamed in agony. 'Good. Now then, Richard, let's see if you've got real balls.'

***

Wen had shared the full story with her team now. Everyone knew that time was running out; that they needed to act, and act fast.

'Nothing so far,' Cassie said. She was beginning to feel defeated. They were getting nowhere, and it was now almost 3 am. If the story played out in real life, they had about an hour before Becky and Richard would be killed. She felt sick, and her head hurt from lack of sleep and reading so much.

She glanced at the page she had just been looking at. Something felt relevant, but what, and why? Cassie read it again, slowly, quietly.

'If they want to find me, they will have to work 24/7.'

She blinked. That was it. 'Ma'am, I think I know where Damian works.'

Wen crossed the incident room to her sergeant. 'Where?'

'Didn't David Lowery say he went into a coffee shop in Stockton Heath called 24/7?'

'I think so. Why?'

Cassie pointed to the sentence she had just read.

'Good girl, Cassie. Get the manager on the phone and find out if the shop has a cellar. If it does, tell him to meet us there.'

***

'Dante,' said Becky. 'You're Dante from the coffee shop.'

He walked slowly towards her, smiling. 'At last. I didn't think you were going to remember. Not that it matters now.' He checked his watch. 'I'm disappointed with your colleagues, I must say. I really did think they would reach you before I killed you both. I left them plenty of clues, but they just weren't clever enough. Sad.'

Becky looked at Richard's bleeding body. He was on a slightly higher level than she was, and his blood dripped down the steps like bright red tears. When Dante had made those last two cuts Richard had howled like a wounded dog, and now he was bleeding out. Blood streamed down his leg, the original spurting reduced to a constant, steady flow. Dante had spots of blood on his face and hands, but he didn't seem to mind at all.

He walked behind Becky. 'It's awful seeing someone you care about in pain, isn't it?' he murmured in her ear. 'But not being able to do anything about it, that's worse. Don't you think?' He slid his hands round her throat, and very gently ran them up and down her neck.

Becky choked back a sob. Was he about to start on her?

'Do you know how long it takes to bleed to death from just a nick in the groin? No? I would have thought you'd know this, Becky. Come on, think!'

Becky wanted to tell him to go fuck himself, but she knew that as long as she could keep him engaged in conversation, she might stay alive. 'Not long, I would have thought.'

'That's not an answer. I want you to tell me exactly how long it will take for a man like Richard to exsanguinate. Minutes? Hours? Not days.'

'Well, it depends on so many different things,' Becky managed to say.

'Good. Now we're getting somewhere. Expand that thesis.'

'Age, health, fitness…'

'Excellent. And Richard is young, healthy and fit.' He walked around to face her again. 'Do you think he's fit?'

'He looks after himself, yes.'

'Yes, but do you think he's *fit*? Do you fancy him?' He glanced at Richard's bleeding, battered body. 'Well, not so much now. When you worked together, I mean. I could have; did you?'

'No, he's a colleague. We just worked together.'

'But you're going to share something very special. Something not many people ever get to do.'

'What?'

'You're going to die together, and that's a privilege. "As I revolved with the eternal twins, I saw revealed, from hills to river outlets, the threshing-floor that makes us so ferocious."'

'What?'

'Beautiful, isn't it. From *The Divine Comedy*. Dante, like me a poet and writer who suffered for his art. I identify with him, I feel his pain. That's why I changed my name to his; we are one spirit.'

Becky could see that this man was in a world of his own making; a terrible world full of pain and hurt. Suddenly he turned back to her. 'Now the other couple, I did them the other way around. He had to watch his lovely wife suffer. That drove him mad with grief, so when I killed him it was a mercy, really.'

'What now?' Becky didn't want the answer she most feared.

'Now we wait for Richard to breathe his last, and then I'll put you out of your misery, Becky. It won't hurt, I promise. I've had my fun for the moment.' He sat down opposite Richard, watching.

'You need help, Dante, you're not well. Let me help you.' It was pathetic, it was desperate, but Becky was out of ideas and time.

'I'm not well?' Dante laughed. 'Look around this room, Becky. I'd say Richard wasn't well, and you don't look too good yourself, but me? I'm just dandy.' Suddenly he stood up. 'I've had enough now.' He picked up his knife, walked over to Richard's dangling body, and slashed his throat.

Becky screamed in horror as the little blood left in Richard's body oozed from the gash in his neck. Then Dante picked up a plastic bag. With three strides he was behind Becky, and the bag was over her face.

Becky felt the bag pull tight around her neck, and his hands twisted the plastic into a hard knot at the back of her head. She gasped in panic, and the plastic contoured to her face like an obscene second skin. She tried to drag in air that wasn't there, her eyes felt as if they would burst out of her head, and everything went black.

29

'Becky, we've got you.'

Words in the distance. Somebody was trying to put something over her mouth. She wrenched at it frantically. 'No, no please!' He was back, and trying to kill her again.

She could smell something metallic; she could taste it in her mouth. Now movement; someone was carrying her. No, she was floating.

Sleep, more voices, pain in her arm that she tried to hit out at. He was back, sticking a knife into her arm. No, she had dreamt that bit, surely. She was moving again, she felt sick, she *was* sick.

Something else pushed into her mouth. Becky fought for a moment, then wondered why she was bothering. He was going to kill her anyway. Why struggle any more?

It was just too much, and she was tired. Sleep, death, there wasn't much difference really.

***

'Hello, sleepyhead.'

Becky opened her eyes a little, scared of what she might see. Her vision was blurred and there was white light; too much white light. Someone brushed against her hand. Fear coursed through her as she flinched and tried to scream.

'Becky, Becky, it's all right. It's me, Elliot. You're safe. You're in hospital.'

She opened her eyes as wide as she could. Elliot was standing over her with a grin like the Cheshire Cat, which didn't do anything to help her state of mind. 'Where is he? Don't let him in!' She looked around the room, searching for evil.

Elliot sat down. 'He's in custody, Becky. He can't hurt you; he can't hurt anyone.'

She turned her head towards him. 'How long have I been here? What happened? How's Richard?' Her voice was strange;

she didn't sound like her.

'You've been here twenty-four hours. They had to sedate you; you were fighting them all the way. How do you feel?'

'Everything hurts,' she admitted. 'How's Richard?'

Elliot took her hand. 'I'm so glad you're all right, Becky. I was going out of my mind.'

'He's dead, isn't he?'

Elliot didn't answer, but she could see from his face that she was right

***

Wen sat in her office, lost in thought, wondering if she could have done something different, secured a better outcome.

The chief inspector had come down with a bottle of whisky after she had charged Damian Anderson, aka Dante Black, with three counts of murder, one of attempted murder, and four counts of false imprisonment.

'Are you OK?' he asked, as he poured a drink into two coffee mugs. She didn't condone drinking at work normally. Wen nodded, and he passed her mug back to her. 'You did a great job, Wen. The whole team did.'

'Not good enough to save Richard, though.' She looked down at the drink, then took a mouthful. It burnt the back of her throat, but she was glad it hurt. She wanted to feel something. Anything.

'He admitted to everything?' Charles Manning asked.

'Yep, he put his hands up to it all. He's proud of what he's done.' Wen closed her eyes as pain ricocheted around her brain.

'What about Martin Grimes? What was his part in it all?' Wen's boss finished his drink and poured himself a second. 'More?' he asked, but Wen shook her head.

'Martin was muscle. Damian Anderson isn't a big man, and he needed help with moving bodies around. Martin was head over heels in love, but even he reached breaking point.'

'Does Dr Baron know what killed Richard?'

'Probably hypovolemia. There was a lot of blood.' Wen

took another sip of whisky. She didn't want to talk about it, but she had to tell her boss what had happened.

'Any idea how he got Richard down there?'

'He told us that he rang Richard, claiming he'd seen a woman being manhandled in the car park at the back of the coffee shop, and said he thought it looked like Becky. So Richard, being Richard, went off to play the hero instead of calling it in. Then he knocked him over the head. There was evidence of blunt force trauma.' Wen drank a little more whisky. 'How was Pauline?' She was relieved she hadn't had to do that visit.

'In a bad way. Her mum came round, and I've left a Family Liaison Officer with them. They were waiting for the doctor when I left.'

'Right. I'll visit tomorrow and pay my respects.'

'And Becky?' Charles looked at Wen very seriously.

'We got there just in time; he'd got a plastic bag over her head. Becky had passed out, and needed CPR to get her breathing.' Wen paused, thinking about it. 'I haven't interviewed Becky yet; she had to be sedated. Her ex is with her, and her mum's on her way from London.'

'Was it him in her house?'

'Yes, it was. It seems David Lowery was being blackmailed by some lowlife who had photos of him that he didn't want posting on the internet. So Lowery got keys copied for him and he burgled houses as the opportunity presented itself. Damian was the go-between, got the keys cut for Lowery for a fee.'

'And he kept a copy of Becky's?'

'He kept copies of all of them. I suspect he'd been in a few houses, finding out about who lived there and what their lives were like, looking for victims.' Wen closed her eyes again, but all she could see was Richard's lifeless body hanging from the post he had been chained to. She opened them and shook her head, trying to get rid of the image that had burnt itself into her retinas.

'Get yourself home, Wen. I don't suppose you'll sleep, but

try and get some rest.'

'Thank you, sir.'

***

Wen pulled into her drive. Another car was there, but she had no idea who it belonged to. How it had got past Aran, the guardian of the house, was even more of a mystery. Surely it wasn't the press?

As she approached the front door it swung open. Jeff was standing there, hands deep in his trouser pockets, looking at her with his head on one side.

She went up to him. 'How did you know?'

'I called him,' said Aran, from behind Jeff. 'I thought you might need someone to talk to, and he owes us, big time.'

Wen felt tears rolling down her face. Her body shook, and as her legs started to give way Jeff had her in his arms. 'It's OK, Wen, it's all going to be OK.'

EPILOGUE

They want to make a film about me, it seems.

I've got an agent now, too. My first book hit the bestseller list, and the second is almost finished.

I have plenty of time to write here. This hospital is all right. And I've been in a few, so I should know.

My creative writing tutor was correct when he said I had talent; the public can't get enough of me.

So I got everything I wanted.

Who's laughing now?

THE VEIN MURDERER

I lay on my bed listening to the traffic going past in the rain. A quiet Whoosh, building up to a sound like the tide coming home, then receding again as the vehicle escaped my hearing. It is almost hypnotic, a rhythm of sound, soothing and repetitive, coming and going.

The pain in my back nags at me, and hot spasms shears through the muscles in my thighs sending pins and needles into my feet. But soon it will be gone, as I wait for my friend to work. Drugs are wonderful things. They take away the fear, make life bearable, so I can function like a normal human being.

Without them? Well, I would fall into a deep black hole, where knifes hack at my soul, fire burns my neurons, where I scream, and scream for it to all end. My private hell. I often wonder if I will wake up again after I've taken it, or will I just go into a peaceful sleep.? Will they find me dead in my bed? And do you know, I don't care! When that sensation of fear and torture wraps itself around my body like a piece of barbed wire being pulled tighter and tighter, I really don't care.

When I beg for more of it, when I would snatch it from the hands of my mother, the mouths of my babies if I had too, I don't care. But then that's what being an addict is, no one else matters, no one.

I feel myself float away now, my muscles are starting to relax, my breathing is easier, my pain recedes just like that last car going past my window, whoosh.

1.

Doctor John Baron stood up and looked at the scene about him. He sighed, tired and disillusioned about life, or to be more accurate, death, John wondered if he should change his career, or at least take a break from it.

On the first floor of the derelict old pub were the bodies of two young adults, locked in each other's arms, for all the world as if they were just asleep. It might have been almost poetic if not for the blow flies invading their cavities showing that they had been dead for at least two days.

Just another drug related death? May be. There was certainly enough drug paraphernalia scattered around the floor, and the female still had a tourniquet around her arm, which was now a slightly deeper shade of grey than the rest of her exposed tissue. But as SOCO's buzzed around the area like the flies on the bodies, John had his doubts, it just didn't feel right.

Yes, Warrington had a growing drug problem, just like everywhere else, but these two? She was well dressed, nice hair, manicured nails. He was scruffier than she, but still not your typical drug taker. He couldn't see any other track marks on their arms, though addicts found many places on their bodies to inject that are hard to detect, unless you knew where to look, and God help him, John knew where to look. Could it be a double suicide, or even murder/ suicide? And why here?

True, this was a well-known squat for the drug taking fraternity, and the policed raided it on a regular basis, closing it down, putting more barbed wire up, bigger padlocks on the doors, thicker wood on the windows. But it only gave the people keen to get back in a greater challenge, which of course they always overcame.

As John waited for Detective Chief Inspector Wen Price to arrive, he could do nothing but speculate. He was the scientific facts guy, she the sleuth that hunted down leads, saw pattens that no one else saw and made leaps of faith that no one else could or would make.

She was the yin to his yang, they worked well together, and if he was brutally honest with himself, which Doctor John Baron wasn't in the habit of doing, he was just a tiny bit in love with her.

ALSO BY THE SAME AUTHOR.

All Manor of People.

Sally thinks she has escaped her sordid past, does she run away again, or does she face the awful truth?

Richard feels he is being punished by being posted to a quiet Cumbrian town, a far cry from the London Met.

Why does Dawn, a teacher at the local high school, and her son, Alex have such a tense relationship?

Emma, the oldest resident shares opinions with her two closest friends, Oliver and Tristan. But they have problems of their own.

All so different. But one thing binds them together, the place where they live, The Manor.

I'll Never Be A Ninja Now!

Step Taylor has a black belt for relationships and is a third Dan in the art of getting involved.

But why has this middle-aged woman retired at such an early age? What has caused her PTSD?

And how did she get mixed up with a suicidal woman? Are the police really going to arrest her?

Read this rollercoaster tale according to the word of Steph, were she looks at her life now, and retrospectively, in this hilarious tale of a modern-day family.

Just a Little Prick

Carol Bissett started nursing at the age of 17 in the late 1960's, finally retiring in 2014.

During those years she had some breaks, emergency stops and did a few three-point turns.

This window into her world, shows the way, we have over the years, treated both nurses and patients. How we view sickness and death, and the ways in which we deal with both.

Sad in parts but written with Carol's irreverent sense of humour, which brings the saying 'life goes on' very much to mind.

WHO IS CAROL BISSETT?

Carol was born in Australia, brought up in Widnes Cheshire, married and moved down the road to Warrington.

After having a family she finished training to be a nurse but has done many other jobs in between.

In the 1990's the family moved to Cumbria, where they stayed for the next 23 years.

Carol has been married for 46 years and has 4 grown up children, two of them still live at home.

Now retired and back in Warrington, she has manged to fulfil a lifetime ambition, to become a published writer.

Writing full time for the last 3 years has enabled her to write and publish 4 books to date.

When not writing and being involved with the writing community, Carol is an avid reader, especially, as you might guess, of crime. Also a self-confessed television addict, on mostly medical and crime themes, always trying to beat the medical team to a diagnosis or the police to solving the murder.

The next Warrington Detective will be available before Christmas this year (2020), and a short taster follows to whet the appetite. Bon appetite!

Printed in Great Britain
by Amazon

49028228R00099